HIDDEN IN DARKNESS

SALVATORE PREPARATORY ACADEMY BOOK 2

ALI D JENSEN

Lux,

Girl, you've been my rock throughout this whole series. You tell me when I write total trash and you support me when I don't feel like I'm good enough. You are such a talented writer and an amazing friend. I'm SO thankful to know you!

Hannah,

To be honest, I'm not really sure how I lived my life without you for so long. Thank you for being my own personal superhero and for guiding me through the unknown obstacles in this crazy adventure that is the book world.

"I must also have a darkside if I am to be whole."
C.G. Jung

ONE

LDJ

MINE. MINE. MINE.

Dannazione! I'm wholly consumed by her. My train of thought leads me to possessiveness. It's overtaking me, making me need to move in and sweep her up off her feet and run far away - *fast*. My brain is on overdrive, caught between obsessing over her and talking myself out of stepping in and killing everyone before taking her back home. I'm fully aware that I'm driving myself to the brink of insanity with all of this bullshit stalking. I'm aware that I've devolved from the imposing threat of my enemies to a raving lunatic stalker. I'm trying exceptionally hard not to be that creepy guy that lurks in the dark to watch his prey; yet I keep finding myself back in this situation, watching mia bella live a life she wasn't supposed to even know about yet. Essentially, I'm becoming borderline compulsive and sociopathic over this girl. While I can see and feel it happening, there's little I can do to stop it. Sono un maniaco - I'm a maniac. Or at least, I'm becoming one. Chi cazzo sono più- who the fuck am I anymore? I don't even recognize myself.

What in the fuck is she doing? She must not be receiving any of my letters or notes. Fottutamente stupido! There's no way she'd be so fucking stupid as to blatantly ignore every warning I've given to her in those notes. She's too smart to put herself in so much danger. Even if she doesn't remember who I am, the notes alone should set off all of the warning signals in her brain. Growing up on the streets of Chicago has given her a clear sense of danger. I'm not exactly well known for my easy temperament and I'm being pushed to my very limits now. I've killed for less and while I'd like to think I'd never do anything to cause her physical harm, but I don't know how much longer I'll be able to reign in my emotions before I react. Watching these bastardi sporchi - filthy bastards, touch *my* girl is torture.

I am a proud Italian-American man, and within me is a wild, often untamable beast that single-handedly causes my emotions to boil over. My bisnonno always called it passione, saying that strong Italian men must know how to revel in their vigorous spirit in any circumstance.

"Che si tratti di amore, perdita, lussuria, odio o celebrazione" He would say - 'be it love, loss, lust, hate, or celebration'.

"Sii un uomo appassionato in tutto ciò che fai," he would tell me. 'Be a passionate man in all you do.' He was one of the best men to have ever lived. His heart of gold transcended this world. He was much different than his son.

My nonno used to tell me that I'm hot-headed and needed to learn to control it; at least up until the day I did and put him in his place. He is a heartless man. He very well may only love my mamma and myself, but even that has its limits. He values cruelty, control and power. He is a made man in every sense of the word.

Mamma tells me I'm melodramatic, knowing I get it from her. I can't help but speak fluent Italian in my speech *and* actions when I feel overwhelmed with intense emotions in the same way she does.

I've long since learned to hide behind a well-crafted facade. Some call it an excellent poker face. Really, I'm overly conscious of the image I present to the world. My persona is one of a cold, calculating killer. A man that resides in the dark and lurks among our enemies to take them out one by one. I personally have more power than I should and with that, I need to be vigilant at all times of myself - and those I surround myself with. Image is everything in my business. More so because of *who* I am and how quickly I rose to power. As the most well-known killer of the Gavino family, I am perceived as that of the devil amongst those who dare speak my name. *Il Diavolo.*

These past months of Quinn not being within my control have been torture and my patience is running thin. It's February now. She's finally getting close to the end of the school year. I was going to let her finish out her high school career to get the diploma she's worked so hard for, but damn if it hasn't been a shit time watching her do it. At this point, I'm not even likely to make it to the end of her junior year.

I've only had to step in a few times throughout her life to clean up some of the messes she's found herself in. I'll never forget my first time murdering a man, because it was *her* I killed for. That was the night I became a made man. That night was the night I lost any notion that I could pretend to have a normal childhood; it was gone, and the irony wasn't lost on me.

The man was rather forgettable, yet his face will forever be burned into my brain. She wasn't more than thirteen at the time when her pretend mother allowed a random, shady fuck into the house. It was likely he was offering some sort of drug for sex. It's who Lauren Davis was at her core - a crackwhore. She didn't bother to care if she was responsible for a child my grandfather placed with her or not. She didn't have enough regard for her own life, let alone Quinn's. My nonno's first mistake was not recognizing that for the danger it was, or maybe not caring. The man had worked his way into their broken home one way or another and used his advantage to get to Quinn. I'd just flown home from Italy and instead of going home, I went straight to her house in the city. I needed to see her - it had been too long since I'd last laid eyes on her. I'd had my regular security detail with me at the time and they had to hold me back when I saw what the man was trying to do.

Lauren must have gotten too high to notice that he'd taken Quinn outside into the poor excuse of a backyard they had. It was a pretty ideal place for what he'd had planned because the overhead light was burnt out. It was more of a slab of concrete than a yard, surrounded by a chain link fence. At the end of the fenced-off property was a walkway that led into a dark alleyway from the other side of the city block. But I could see everything from where I stood in the dark, seething under the light of the full moon as I watched him throw her out the door and overpower her with his weight and size.

At first, she started to fight in an attempt to wriggle her way out of his hold. Never once did she even make a single noise. No screaming for help, no yelling or crying... And then as if accepting her fate, she stopped moving altogether. She laid perfectly still like she was going to just lay down and allow him to take advantage of her. I couldn't believe the sight before me.

Only a pathetic, insecure man would need to force himself on such a small girl. I was vibrating with rage, held back by the arms of my favorite security guard and mentor. The disgusting excuse of a man held her down on the wet, broken concrete that made up the strip of land behind their house and ripped her shirt down the middle. Puberty must have started for her while I was away in Italy because I remember noticing that she'd started developing breasts by that point, her curves becoming decidedly more noticeable. Two of my guards continued to stay back with me, and two of them silently moved towards the sickening scene before me. It all felt like it was happening in slow motion.

My guys had almost reached them when Quinn did the unimaginable. The man had been too distracted to realize that while she was playing dead, he'd given her the advantage by releasing her to remove his own clothing. My eyes stayed glued to her as she drew her knee up as hard as she could and destroyed the man's balls, while simultaneously driving her small fist into his Adam's apple, completely disarming him. Even as small as she was, she was already smart enough to know her advantages in attacking such sensitive areas of the body with as much force as she could muster. I was so incredibly proud of her, even while fuming that she'd ever had to be put in that position in the first place. It felt like it was all my fault. Guilt and hatred overwhelmed me in that moment more than ever before.

Assuming this wasn't the first time she'd had to protect herself and it likely wouldn't be the last, she almost had me taking her back home with me that very night. If it weren't for la famiglia, I would have. Nonno would've whipped me for putting the family in danger, and out of spite he would've ended her life. And possibly mine. My hands were tied.

When the asshole rolled off of her in pain, she made a run for it and back into her house. I'm not sure if she locked the door behind her or not, but I didn't care. It didn't matter. The piece of shit was never going to lay his hands on her again - or anyone else. She would be safe - for now. My men crept along the shadows, picked him up off the ground, and dragged him back to me.

My mentor, Piero continued to keep his hold on me, squeezing his large palm on my shoulder. He silently reminded me to reel in my crazy temper and be smart about what would happen next. Of all my men, he has always been my most trusted. Whenever my grandfather couldn't be with me, he was. His job at the time was the enforcer role within la famiglia and he taught me everything I know. It wasn't always easy being in my position with most of the men surrounding me being much older than me, but he never questioned whether or not I deserved the role I'd been thrusted into. For that, he'll always have my loyalty.

I remember the moment he handed me his gun with a silencer already on it like it was yesterday. Without hesitation, I took aim right between the scumbags frightened eyes. I watched as his lips quivered in fear, seeing the motion of his lips begging for his life but not hearing the words come from his mouth. It was as though I was seeing everything in slow motion. The sweat that beaded at his temple dripped down his face and intermingled with his tears.

"You never should've touched her. *Signore Gesù Cristo, figlio di Dio, abbi pietà di me peccatore.*" my whispered breath lingering in the space surrounding us. My threat and conscience clear, I sent my prayers for forgiveness to the holy spirit as my bisnonno taught me, though I was unable to make my voice loud and commanding as the head Gavino would've preferred.

The moment I shot him; I knew that it forever cemented me to my nonno's world. I'd never escape this life. At that point, I didn't care as long as I was able to have Quinn by my side one day. I knew she would make all of this worth it. She's always been the light to my dark. The goodness in my nights and the reason my heart beats. Even at a young age, I knew she was the most important thing to ever happen to me.

It's basically my fault she's had to live the life she has and every second of every day, it has been the source of my anger. She's been the driving force behind me moving up the ranks so quickly. Admittedly, I've remained single-mindedly focused. I'd much rather have had her with me all this time but it was too risky. Too dangerous. But now, the real danger lies in me having to continue to wait for what's mine. Alessandra Evelyn Quinn Salvatore is *mine* and there's not a thing anyone can fucking do about it. I will have her within my grasp again and this time I will keep her.

She's going to be my wife. It was a deal signed in blood between families several times over and no one will get away with taking her from me, especially not *him*. She was never supposed to come back here - at least not without me being the most important man in her life first. She was never supposed to learn of her life this way. It was supposed to go according to my fucking plan, but no, some dipshit had to fuck up and mess everything up. Now I'm here, neglecting most of my duties for the Gavino's, watching amore della mia vita - the love of my life, parade around with three other fucking guys. Three guys who clearly worship the ground she walks on. Just because I understand it, doesn't mean I'll fucking tolerate it. I've done the same her whole life, mostly from a distance, because I wasn't allowed to be publicly affiliated with her, but that shit's about to end. She's fucking mine. Mi amore. My sweet, beautiful love. I've already been cheated out of our whole lives together up 'til now. I refuse to be cheated out of our future.

And now I'm going to come off as il furfante. I'll be painted the bad guy and I know there's no other way for it to go down. I just need her to see-to understand where I'm coming from. She'll understand once she knows our history. I have to believe in that, because she's too important to me to let her walk away and fall in love with these three men who, in all fairness, are not altogether different from me.

They aren't me though, and they can't have her. I won't let them. I won't be screwed out of the life I always imagined I'd have. I worked my ass off for it, and these fuckwits came in and foolishly fell for the wrong girl, *my* irresistible girl. I can't kill them without serious blow back so I'll have to find another way. One way or another, she'll be mine again. At this rate it's bound to happen sooner rather than later.

TWO

LDJ

MY TEXTS SEEM to have woken her up. I knew she hadn't been reading my notes, otherwise none of this would've even been a problem. It's well into March now and I've watched all along since she's been here these last several months. I've watched her grow into her own power and seen the glow radiate from within her as she learns her place in our world. She has always been the light in the dark, but now she shines so bright, even the darkest demons can't compete with her brilliance. She's a queen among men and she's allowed herself three strong kings to accompany her as she navigates through her upcoming role as a leader, an underboss. Eventually meant to be *La Don*.

Climbing quickly up the ranks to join her grandfather at his side. She's everything I hoped she would become. She's just done it in the wrong place. She's meant to be by *my* side. Once she'd accepted that we belong together, that's when she was meant to make her entrance into the world she was so cruelly ripped away from. Together we were meant to merge the East and West coast and rule with a strong unified hand. Now I have to play stupid games to chase her away from the life she's grown to love and take her back into my arms. Plus,

I have to hope that she doesn't fight too hard to get away from me. My jealousy has overwhelmed my good sense and I can't wait any longer.

I sent her some shitty text messages two days ago and now my men and I are tailing her across the United States. I can only imagine she's going back to Chicago to figure out who's behind all of the secret messages. Honestly, it felt all kinds of wrong to do everything so mysteriously, but I have to protect the administration as well. Especially since I've been more neglectful of my station in La Cosa Nostra than ever before.

I'll have to send someone over to her old house to clean up any messes and to set up something special for her. Although, I'd like to leave her another handwritten note so I may need to let my security detail take over tailing her and fly out to set something up myself. Hmm. that actually sounds like a better plan.

Calling up Piero, who I left in my place while I've been living in the shadows of Northern California, I fill him in on my plan and make my way to the nearest airport, knowing he'll make sure the rest of the guys I had with me stay with Quinn.

By the time my driver pulls up to the airport, I've already gotten a team to go clear out the old shack of a house she grew up in, making sure all of the squatters have been kicked out. They are set to clean up her room and set the scene I've requested. I also have a seamstress rush order a custom-designed wedding gown for my girl to leave for her so she has a full understanding of what is about to happen.

"Hi! Welcome to Northwest Air, how can I help you?" A young blonde woman greets me, fluttering her fake eyelashes flirtatiously once she takes a good look at my face.

"I'd like the next available flight to Chicago." I tell her, in no mood to waste time.

"Oh, why the need to go so far away?" She pouts.

"I'd love to help, is this for business or *pleasure*?" She purrs, her question heavy with innuendo as she starts licking her glossy lips. She looks me over from head to toe like she wouldn't mind me whipping my dick out and fucking her here on her workstation.

"Just get me a ticket. I don't have time for this and you aren't my type. First class. Chicago. Immediately. Find the ticket." I say, growling out my annoyance. Although, I *do* take some pleasure in her shock at my statement. She's not an ugly girl and I imagine she doesn't get turned down very often.

"Of course sir, I'm... I'm so sorry." She has enough sense to look embarrassed, stuttering and shifting her gaze down to type quickly to find me what I need.

"It looks like we have a flight out in thirty minutes but you'd be pushing your luck for time with the security line if you have any baggage."

"The timeline will be fine. I have loads of baggage, but no luggage. I'll take the ticket." I say, handing her my debit card and ID.

"Have a lovely day and good luck, sir," she says, handing me back my cards along with my plane ticket.

I make my way through security fairly quickly since I have nothing with me other than my wallet and phone and get to my boarding gate just in time for them to call for priority seating to board the plane. Handing over my ticket to the attendant I get another heated glance sent my way, hiding none of the attraction she feels toward me. These bitches are fucking thirsty today.

I get this a lot. I'm by no means ugly. I'm not self-centered or anything, but I'm also not delusional enough to pretend like I didn't win the genetics lottery. I'm what some would call classically tall, dark and handsome, but with a sinister twist. Tattoos cover a large percentage of my body, mostly to hide some of my battle scars and typically in places I can cover in my suits. Raffaele Gavino isn't much of a fan and before bisnonno died, he couldn't stand to look at them either. I've tried to remain fairly respectful of that. My piercings didn't go over well with anyone at first either, but oh fucking well.

I'm one hundred percent not interested in anyone that isn't Quinn. When she touches me while handing me my boarding pass, lingering and tracing her fingers along mine, my whole body stiffens. I slowly pull my hand back with a glare aimed her way.

"Not gonna happen," I growl out, unwilling to hold back the disgust in my voice. I watch her face redden and take a small amount of pleasure in her embarrassment, before moving to take my seat on the plane. I belong to one woman and only one woman. And she may not know it yet, but she belongs to me.

I don't want or need anyone else touching me. It's common amongst the mafia for men of power to have wives *and* mistresses, girlfriends, or toys on the side. I'm not that kind of guy. Quinn is it for me and I'm okay with that. I just hope she is too.

As I write the note I'm leaving behind for Quinn, I realize how disturbingly nauseating I'm coming across. Seeing the words in print is bone-chillingly disgusting. To an extent, I need this to be the case. I have to make her understand the reality of what's to come and also hopefully throw her off my scent a little bit. Maybe when she finally meets me, she'll notice that I'm not as bad as the letters, notes, and texts make me out to be. Well, I am, but never to her. Even I've noticed how badly I've made myself out to be, but what's done is done. I'm not a good guy. I'm not nice or sweet or kind. I'm a killer. I'm an underboss for the goddamn mafia.

My grandfather *is* the mafia. La Don of all the Eastern territories and the head of the Gavino family. There is no coming back from that. I can't make myself deserving of the love I'm so desperate for.

I finish the note and lay it down next to the gown specifically designed for mia bella. This dress is made for her deadly curves - I swear her wicked body was made for sin. The lace shows more skin than I'd typically like others to see but there's no doubt in my mind that she'll look stunning in it, provided I can get her to willingly put it on and walk down the aisle. I know what a spitfire my girl is and I'm prepared for the worst of things. I'm not beyond forcing her hand, though I'd prefer her to actually want me.

Once I set up all of the candles and lay everything out for her, I leave. I don't want to watch this part. Knowing she wants nothing to do with me and seeing it are two different things. I'm not sure my heart or my ego can take the rejection. I'm a ruthless, sometimes downright evil guy, but with her I seem to turn to goo. I always have and I don't think I'm capable of witnessing her find these things and hating me for it. Because she *will* hate me. It's inevitable. I'm about to take her back and there's nothing anyone can do to stop me. Not even Matteo, Cohen or Noah. I know they're tailing her. They'd have been stupid not to.

Unfortunately for them, the odds are stacked in my favor. They know little to nothing. I've laid out some breadcrumbs for them to learn the truth but honestly, by then I'll already have my girl and they'll be too late. Like I said, I know I'm the villain in our story and I'm okay with that as long as Quinn is willing to learn the truth and can accept me for all that I am, and all that we will be. After all, this is all for her.

THREE

LDJ

I GET in my car and drive to meet up with Piero. We have to plan her kidnapping and while it's necessary, it's also annoying. I own almost everyone in Chicago so it won't be hard. It all just feels like a necessary evil. I loathe the idea of hurting her or making her fear or hate me. I know it is going to happen whether I like it or not, but still. Who in their right mind enjoys the love of their life despising them? Even with all the stalking and creepiness, I'm still of sound mind despite the image I've created for myself.

"Piero, my friend." I speak into my phone, knowing he won't greet me when I call.

"Can you send a team to the island to set up the cellar? I'm on my way to you so we can plan the best way to take her. I'd like to handle this all by the end of the day. We will be staying on the island to ensure privacy and our safety as we navigate through the worst of our reunion. She won't like what is about to happen and we need every precaution in place so she can't run before I make her see what's meant to be. I won't tolerate disobedience in this situation."

"And you think imprisoning her in the cellar is the best choice?"

He grumbles, clearly upset that this is all happening. He's never truly liked Quinn. He sees her as my one and only weakness. He's not wrong, but he foresees her being the administration's ultimate downfall.

"For the time being. Yes. There needs to be a punishment before she can enjoy the comforts of the estate. Her choices as of late have been borderline scandalous and to be honest, I may need to break her before we can begin building our life together. Though I'll marry her by force if necessary at this point. Also, make sure the bare minimum staff is on at the estate. I will be taking care of her myself. We will need guards stationed of course, but otherwise let's keep things as secretive as possible for now," I say, knowing it will get back to my grandfather. He'll assume there's a violent undertone in my meaning. He's nothing if not ruthless. Had it not been for my mamma's presence in my life, I'd likely be the same way. As far as the world and my nonno know, I am.

"Fatto, non sarà un problema." He lets me know that it will be handled without any problem.

"Grazie, see you soon." I say, before hanging up and driving in peaceful silence. Everything is finally coming back together and life will be good again. At least after dealing with Quinn's wrath. That'll be the hard part.

MAKING my way down the back alley behind the restaurant part of the hotel Quinn is staying at, I adjust my mask so that none of my face is showing. I'm covered head to toe in black to blend into the shadows. This hotel is owned by my family, as is about seventy nine percent of Chicago; the rest mostly is bought and paid for when necessary for business. The cameras are all being manipulated by my IT team and none of the staff will pay me any mind as I sneak around. Most of them are on my payroll, but as seen at the time of

Lauren's death, not all of them. I'll still err on the side of caution in case a guest of the hotel sees me and starts feeling chatty with the police. I'd rather this go smoothly, even if I have to look the part of a robber to do so. I'm completely unidentifiable right now and that's how it'll stay.

"She's in her room now. We placed her on the first floor for easy access. She's in the Princess Suite." My security detail tells me in my earpiece.

Of course they put her in the Princess Suite - how fitting. The hotel itself is a bit ostentatious, yet with that comes the comfort of having a suite for each floor. The building isn't meant to only have the one penthouse suite for the wealthy. It gives multiple choices to display your wealth when choosing a location to stay for business or pleasure.

I make my way toward her room and produce my master key card from my pocket. Using it to gain access to her room, I watch the red light turn green and open the door to the entryway into her suite. I watch for movement as I walk into the open space of her lounge area and when I see none, I realize that she must be in the bedroom. I know that Matteo was in here setting up security cameras not that long ago, so I need to be fast.

Pulling the needle from my pocket and uncapping it, I make my way to her bedroom door, silently twisting the knob. I finally see my dark haired beauty just as she's hanging up her cell phone. She must have checked in with Alessandro and Cecelia if I had to guess. She pockets her phone and stares out her window contemplatively not realizing I'm behind her until she sees my reflection in the window. She tries to turn and face me, gasping when I grab her by her midsection and hold down her arms. Being as careful as I can, I place the needle into her neck, allowing the drugs to take effect. Almost immediately, she becomes dead weight in my arms and I place a dark covering over her face in case we're seen leaving. I shift her into a fireman carry and with lightning speed, move out of the building.

Right when I get to the SUV, Matteo bursts out of the building, rage consuming him, but he's too late. We're already making our way down the road and soon we'll be lost on the island. There will be no way to track her. She's finally mine again and now that she's in my arms, I may never let her go.

FOUR

ALESSANDRA

DRIP... Drip... Drip...

I watch each droplet of water slowly leak from one of the cracks in the ceiling next to my bed. It's damp and musty in here - cold too. I have a small piece of thin fabric that I've been using as a blanket when it gets too bad. I've lost count of how many days I've been locked away in this cellar, but it has to be around two weeks or so, maybe longer. It's hard to tell when there's only a tiny window in the heavy wooden door that lets a small sliver of light in. I can hear a brutal storm raising hell outside the stone walls, the rain and thunder echoing throughout the frigid, empty space. It's been going on for several days now, like the weather is somehow in tune with my fucked up mood. I've been struggling to eat. I'm too fucking mad and if it were possible to wear out cement, I'd have done it already with all the pacing I've done in this shithole.

I don't know where the hell I am but I can tell we're somewhere near a coastline. If I had to guess based on my last known location, I'd say somewhere along the East coast but who knows how many days I was drugged and unconscious before I ended up here. The air smells vaguely of saltwater and seaweed, but also of dampness and whatever mold lives down here. So far, the only person that I've seen is a large man that brings me the bare necessities for survival.

In a way, he's been taking care of me, if you can call it that. He feeds me, sure. He also ignores the fuck out of me. He stays long enough to listen when I talk to him, but never responds. It's like he's content to listen to me ramble on, even though I don't often have anything nice to say. I can only imagine he's heard worse.

He's tall and broad - muscular too. He's always got on a tight black shirt that stretches along the large span of his chest; his arms decorated in mesmerizing black ink down to his wrists but he never gets close enough that I can see the intricate designs. He wears black cargo pants and black combat boots. He even has a black mask covering his face and neck. His build rivals that of my guys.

My guys...

Just thinking about them makes me feel a pain so intense, I might as well have cut the limbs from my body. It feels as though my heart has been torn from my body and left for me to watch the blood seep from the wounded organ, as I watch it slowly stop beating.

My three beautifully damaged boys turned into men too soon. It's unfair that each of us have had to grow up before our time. I'm finding myself more and more resentful of that as I'm stuck here, left to think of little else. We all should be living it up as teenagers, causing shenanigans and making mistakes, but that's never been any of our lives. We're all basically adults living in teenagers' bodies, forced to learn and adapt to our lifestyle. It'll never be fair for us; our world is too dark and dangerous.

Fuck, I miss them. My thoughts of them are basically the only thing that keep me from giving up down here. I miss Matteo and his brooding stare, trademark scowl, and deep grumbling voice. I miss Noah's silly antics, sex crazed libido, and hidden depths. I miss Cohen and his quiet strength, creative genius, and intuitive soul. I miss *them* and I know they miss me. I swear, I can practically feel them mourning my loss. They are as much a part of me as this useless heart of mine.

It was stupid of me not to include them on my trip. I know this. I should've just trusted them with my secrets and worked out a plan with them. My need to protect them outweighed my sense of self preservation, so I can't say that I regret that part at all. I *am* starting to regret not allowing them the option to choose whether it was worth the risk to them. If I had, maybe this could've all been avoided. Fuck, maybe we'd still be together right now. I know they must be furious with me. I'm pissed at myself for them. How selfish am I though that *these* are my thoughts? They are safe from whatever this shit is. For that, I can't be anything other than proud of my decision, even if it hurts like a bitch.

Reaching up, I rub at my chest, wishing like hell I still had my heart necklace, the one that I had made to match the guys' watches I got them on Valentine's Day. At some point, I'd been stripped down and put into a silk nightgown set. It's completely contradictory to this shitty place I've been stuck in. Why give me fine silks to sleep in if I'm supposed to sleep in a dank, moldy cellar on a sheet less mattress?

I can't decide if I have a legitimate escape plan yet. Every single day, when the masked man brings me food, I attempt to talk to him and he gives me nothing in return. I've tried everything from yelling at him and cursing him out to attempting to bribe him for information. The guy talks about as much as the stone walls surrounding me. The food here is decent though, wherever *here* is. Aside from that, I have a dingy twin sized mattress on an old wrought iron bed frame and a small table with a battery operated lantern, an itchy piece of fabric for a blanket, and a literal pot to piss in.

I've not been given another set of clothes so this thin silk is getting pretty grimy. It's nasty. No showers means I smell like a dirty asshole. My hair is knotted and oily. Ugh, I can't even *think* about my teeth without gagging. Even at the shittiest of times growing up on the streets of Chicago, I've never felt so physically dirty.

Hearing the door open, I roll over on the mattress, away from the stone wall and toward the man in the mask.

"Hmm... It's you again. Any chance you'll talk to me today?" I ask, knowing I'll get nothing in response. I don't even care - if he's my only option, I'll have a conversation with him anyway.

"So, I don't know if you can smell that stank ass, trash-like smell, but uh, that's me. Any chance we can bounce outta this cavernous dungeon thing so I can take a shower and maybe put on some real clothes?" I ask, lifting an eyebrow in question.

No response. Not even a nod or head shake. He's just staring at me now, his eyes glowing in the surrounding darkness. It's even darker where he's standing but there's still an odd sense of familiarity in them. Even still, there's something ominous lingering in the space around him. This man is dangerous. It seeps from his pores and fills the air around him. He gives off the vibes of a man torn between right and wrong. I don't know if he's working for someone or if he's the one who's been sending me all the creepy roses, but with every meal comes another long stemmed black rose so I know that I'm right where I'm wanted by my secret admirer.

"Seriously man, you may not have noticed but it's kinda cold down here and there's legit no way this thin as fuck silk is doing the trick to keep me from eventually getting hypothermia. All I'm asking for is a hot shower and some real clothes. C'mon, you have to know how fucked up it is to keep me here, right?" I damn near beg. I'm officially pathetic. I don't even want to know me right now. I almost don't even want to *be* me.

"You clearly don't want me to die, or you wouldn't be checking in on me and feeding me every day. I won't even try to escape. Just fucking help me not smell like the rotting corpse of a dead animal. You can't have gone to all the trouble of kidnapping me just to let me rot down here... Right?" I blink up at him, hoping like hell he'll find it in him to care enough to help me. At this point I just need to do what

I can to find an opening out of here. If I can just get out of this creepy cave basement, I can check out my surroundings and figure out a way to get back home. My mom and nonno must be freaking the hell out, given I haven't checked in with them since I got to my hotel in Chicago.

The masked man sets a tray of food on my little side table, turning to walk away from me. *Again.* I can't let that happen so I move as fast as I can, which is admittedly much slower than normal, given how worn out I am from being down here.

Reaching out to grab his arm, only to catch his hand instead, I yank as hard as I can. When my skin touches his, there's a spark of electricity that shoots through my veins, fire burning through me at a simple touch. It makes no sense to me. He's the big, bad masked man. Not to mention, for obvious reasons, I shouldn't be reacting to anyone like this.

I jerk my hand back quickly but the damage is done. He felt it too. His mask covers his face but his eyes are visible and they tighten as though I've pained him. They appear to be black but that may just be the darkness that blankets us in the dull gloom that shadows this cellar. There's something in his gaze though - an overwhelming sense of familiarity that offers a reassuring comfort to settle my nerves when I lock eyes with him. Why, when I look into them does it feel like home? It's momentarily paralyzing. Can this be Stockholm Syndrome? Can someone even develop that in such a small amount of time? What in the actual fuck is happening to me?

"Please," I whisper, showing a vulnerability I know I shouldn't.

Without warning, he grabs me by my arms and starts to move back to my bed. My sense of self-preservation kicks in and I try to fight him off but he's already got a hold of me, and with his size and weight, he easily overpowers me. His grip tightens with each of my own combative movements as I try to fight him off. I let my body go lax in an attempt to throw him off by making him drag my dead weight. Sparks or no sparks, I don't want to let him take me to a bed of any kind. I didn't survive this long just to be raped in some dungeon-cellar-turned-bedroom for a captive. I don't care if I felt a goddamn blazing inferno light me up from within or if I've suddenly developed some form of temporary mental illness. I will *not* let him take advantage of me.

No one but my guys will have me physically. I belong to *them*. I may not have my necklace, my knife, or my gun, but I'm no dummy and I know how to fight. I've done it my whole damn life. With all the power I have left in me, I shove him off of me and move to kick him in his kidneys.

Instead he grabs my foot and yanks me to his body. It's like he can anticipate all of my movements. What the fuck? It's as if he knows me. Using the momentum of my body coming towards his, he moves his hand upward to grab my thigh. With his other hand, he snatches my other leg so I end up wrapped around his waist. I move to shove myself off by pushing at his chest and trying to drop my legs, but he's got a firm hold on me now. He's had the upper hand from the get go and I'm running out of options.

"No! Let *go* of me!!" I scream.

He grunts in response while slamming me onto the bed, coming down on me with the full force of his weight. My worst nightmare has always been someone getting me into this position. He's pressed up tight against my body, his hips moving against mine while he wrestles me into submission from in between my legs. My body instantly locks up. I stop trying to fight him because I'm only making the situation worse by bucking my hips into his. I can feel him harden against my stomach and I become nauseous with worry, but I refuse to let him see me scared. He can have my anger and my fight. He doesn't get to have my fear.

Hatred seeps into my veins as I think of all the ways I'll make him pay if he touches me. I don't care if I die in the process. If he rapes me, I *will* kill him.

Reaching out with one of his giant hands, he clasps my wrists together above my head. Keeping my body locked down with his own, he uses his other hand to pull a set of handcuffs from one of the utility pockets in his cargo pants and locks them onto my wrists, binding me to one of the iron rails at the head rest.

I mindlessly thrash my body around, doing my best to ensure he can't stay near enough to touch me. My movement causes the cuffs to cut into my wrists with how tightly they are clasped onto me. I can feel the sharp bite of the metal and a small trickle of blood moves down my arms, but that's the least of my concerns. I continue to kick and fight with the rest of my body but it doesn't seem to phase the masked man. He steps back and watches me, making no moves to touch me again.

Instant relief floods my entire being at his distance. It appears as though he doesn't want to force himself on me, but what *does* he want? Maybe he's just trying to get me to think he doesn't want me? I felt his dick. I know he's turned on.

"Why are you doing this?" I ask, genuinely confused as to what's going on. When he doesn't respond once again, I start raging.

"What are you going to do? Rape me? Because I'll cut your tiny little dick off before I let that happen, you piece of shit!! I fucking dare you to touch me again! One way or another, I'll find my way out of this. When that day comes, I'm going to fucking destroy you and everything you love." I'm snarling at this point. Yelling and kicking, baring my teeth like a wild animal. I'm almost convinced that I'm losing my mind.

It's not like me to lash out in anger. Typically I use it to *calmly* fuel my fire and gain the upper hand. No. This is *fear*. Pure, unfiltered fear, causing me to lash out and lose my cool. I need to reel it the fuck in and gain some control.

"The only thing I love is you, mia bella." He whispers in a low growl, turning his face from me, like he can't stand to see me this way. His voice sends goosebumps down the length of my body. It looks as though it hurts him to see me so hateful.

Something in his voice triggers me. It stops me dead, mid thrash, and I'm suddenly lost in my own thoughts, trapped in my own memories. At least it feels like a memory, or maybe a dream.

It sounds so familiar, but not... There's something off about it. There's a hint of an accent but also something else, something I can't put my finger on. It's like I'm stuck in a hypnotic-like trance as I let his words sink in and before I can get a full grasp on what's happening, the masked man walks out the door.

FIVE

ALESSANDRA

"OHH FUCK, MY HEAD." I reach up and clasp my hands to my head in an unsuccessful attempt to stop the aching, only to realize I'm no longer handcuffed to the metal bars on the bed, though there are painful marks left behind. My mouth feels so dry and my eyelids are so heavy, they feel like they could be holding the weight of an elephant.

I make a half-hearted attempt to peel open my eyes but the light in the room is blinding and painful. Where's the light coming from? I grab for my makeshift blanket to pull over my head to stop the awful light from making my headache worse, only the fabric isn't rough and itchy. It isn't small either. I grasp a hold of thick, warm, buttery soft sheets and what has to be a feather down comforter. I try to peek one eye open to see what's going on and even though it still hurts, my eyes shoot open wide at the sight before me.

"What the fuck?" I whisper to myself.

Looking around, there's a vast difference to the filthy, damp cellar I'd been residing in for the better part of the last month. Even as everything is spinning a bit, I see that the room I'm in is as large, if not larger than my room at home. The walls are a beautiful light coffee coloring with dark wooden accents. I'm lying on a comfortable king size four poster bed, with cream bedding. There's a delicate ivory lace fabric draped over the bed tied to the posts on each corner of the bed. Next to the bed are two bedside tables, matching beautifully with the chestnut and cream decor. On the table closest to me, I see two Tylenol tablets and a glass of water sitting on top of a note. And no surprise here, there's another long stemmed black rose.

Ugh, I don't even want to touch the note. My head hurts so bad that I'm desperate for the pain pills though. Going against my better judgement, I pick up the note after I swallow the pills and down the entire cup of water. I shouldn't have drank it so fast, because now I feel queasy as shit. The note doesn't help at all. If anything, I think it makes things worse. Nausea swims through my sour stomach, lurching violently with every line I read on the paper.

Ciao mi amore,

I am so very sorry for your most recent accommodations. I hate that I've upset you so deeply. My desire has never been to hurt you. However, there needed to be a punishment for your taking up resi-dence with three other men. I sent you warning after warning and you still allowed them to touch what is mine. You were never theirs to fall in love with. You were given to me when you were just a small girl and I intend to keep you. I fell in love with you years ago and haven't once stopped. Not even while you disobediently engaged with those other men. I don't take kindly to losing and I am not patient enough to wait for you to stop hating me to move things along. I am a busy man and can no longer afford to take the time it requires to tend to you myself. Rest assured, you'll have all of your needs met with our butler, maids and chefs. There are bodyguards throughout the estate as well as at your door. Do not attempt to leave. Do not attempt to run. You will not succeed. I am not a man to make angry, mia bella, so please don't make things harder than they need to be. Take the pain pills on the table and drink a lot of water. You need to rehydrate after being drugged. I wish it hadn't come to that, but I had to get you to your room. You have not yet earned the privilege of knowing our location or seeing the grounds. For the time being you will stay in your room. Only once you've proven yourself worthy will you be allowed out. Until then, you can do your best to prove your loyalty to me - to us. Our wedding is coming up in the late summer months and I'd like to spend some time with you beforehand so you can get to know me, but that will not happen unless you earn it. You have access to food, clothing and books. If you need anything else, let your maids know and they will pass along the message. You have an ensuite bathroom to tend to all of your bathing needs. I heard you loud and clear, mi amore, and I will do everything in my power to ensure your every need is met going forward, you only need to ask. In time, I think you will learn to love me. However, you should never assume I will rape you again. I would never hurt you out of anger or spite, only for pleasure, yours and mine. By the time we become lovers, it will be because your desire is so strong you can't help yourself. Your virtue is to stay intact until our wedding night otherwise. I'm nothing if not capable of waiting for you. Another thing, I won't tolerate your desire to fight me. There are repercussions to your actions and you are rightfully mine to touch as I please. I will only say this one last time. Do not push me, mi amore. Just don't. Ti amo. mia bella. Be good so we can meet properly.

Xo,
LDJ

Fucking gross. Instantly I regret not tearing up the note before reading it like I had when he was sending the notes to me at home. Of course, like always, I had to let my curiosity get the better of me. Fuck, I hate this.

Oh, god. I'm going to throw up.

Making a run for the door next to me, I push through and spot the toilet just in time to empty the very few contents of my stomach into it. I don't know if it's a blessing or a curse that I've been eating so minimally since being locked away in the cellar.

Wiping my mouth with the back of my hand, I stand up and look around, spotting a new toothbrush and toothpaste still in the packages on the counter. I grab them and brush my teeth for the first time in weeks. It feels so good, I may never stop.

I look around and see the shower, so I start it while continuing my quest for spotless teeth, turning the water as hot as I can possibly stand it. I do a quick perimeter check for bugs or cameras before finally stripping down and moving into the scalding hot water.

When I finally finish up with my teeth, I reach for the shampoos and soaps, noticing everything is my signature magnolia scent. I wash my hair twice, scrubbing it aggressively, before I move onto a deep condition and to scrub the excess filth off of my body. I must be close to taking layers of my own skin off because my whole body starts to ache with the desperate cleansing I'm giving myself.

I can feel the hot tears as they trail down my face, it's not natural for me to cry, and I haven't even done so until now. I miss my guys now more than ever. I know I can't sit and stew in my own self-pity. I'm made of tougher stuff than that but it's always just been me to worry about. I've never had other people to care about and the weight of their loss is suffocating me. It hurts. It hurts so bad that my entire being feels broken.

I give myself over to the pain and sorrow I'm feeling. I allow the depression to take over for a while, sinking to the floor of the shower, openly sobbing and curling myself into the smallest form I can. It feels as though I'll completely fall apart if I don't physically hold myself together. This is a whole new side of myself, that I'm far less familiar with. I must need this though because the tears just won't stop.

This continues until the water runs cold. I pull myself up, wrap myself in a towel and drag myself back to my new bed. Too emotionally exhausted to bother even looking for clothes. Knowing at some point I'll have to pull myself together, probably sooner rather than later but for now, I'll continue to grieve. Grieving the loss of my mom and my nonno alone feels so damaging I can barely stand it.

I'm grieving the loss of SB, my best friend. My sister. The only friend I think I've ever actually had. I'm grieving the loss of my determined Matteo, my fierce Noah, and my loyal Cohen. The three guys who own my entire heart and soul. The three men who know me inside and out.

I know I'll find them again someday but in order to escape this place, in order to survive, I'll need to play along, which means I'll need to let them go for now. Knowing this, I give myself over to my grief and when I wake up tomorrow, I'll play this game better than anyone ever could. Tomorrow, I'll be the perfect little queen to this masked king. I'll own his heart, mind, body and soul and then I'll bury him six feet fucking under.

With that thought, I fall into a dreamless sleep.

SIX

ALESSANDRA

FOR THE FOLLOWING WEEK, I'm on point with my good girl routine. I wake up and shower. I dress myself in the luxurious satins and silks left for me in my closet, it's total bullshit that there are no actual clothes, just lingerie and silken nightgowns. At some point I'll need to talk to someone about that. I'm supposedly here to marry some self-entitled prick, one that sounds possessive on a crazy level that may exceed that of Matteo. He can't want me wandering around in front of his guards in panties, right?

I make myself as presentable as possible and when the maids come in, I keep myself perfectly pleasant, making sure to use my manners and not ask for too much. I've been allowed books to read and paper to write on, apparently the pen and paper is just in case I'd like to send notes to the masked man but I honestly can't find it in me to do so just yet. One of the few requests I've made is for the information in regard to my studies. At this rate, I'll be able to graduate this summer. The staff has done an excellent job of keeping me up to date with my school requirements. Although, I imagine school will be out soon enough for summer. It has to be close to the end of April by now if it's not already.

I do what I can to get back into fighting shape by working out, which isn't easy without weights, training bags or anywhere to run, but I do what I can with some basic floor workouts and shadowboxing. My main goal is to get my strength back up so when I have the chance, I'll be able to have a real chance at escaping. I'll bide my time, but at some point in the near future, I'll be free as a bird.

My days are freaking boring for the most part, but a decent portion of the books I've requested are also fun reads so between that and my shitty workouts, it's not all that different from my previous life in Chicago. It seems I'm destined to be a prisoner to my own life no matter where I am. At least this place is clean and I don't have creeps trying to pick me up on every street corner.

My next goal is to gain access to the house I'm staying in and eventually the house grounds, and if nothing else, maybe the internet. I'm not quite on SB or Cohens level but I can do some minimal hacking to try and reach out to someone from my real life.

Knock, knock.

"Come in!" I yell from my bed, my face buried in a physics book.

I don't bother to look up, assuming it's one of the maids bringing me food.

"Ahem" I hear a gruff voice, interrupting my thoughts, causing me to snap my attention towards an older gentleman.

"Hello, Miss Salvatore. My name is James. I'm the butler here at the manor and I've been told to escort you throughout the house to give you a tour. It seems you've done quite well to earn some privileges." The old man speaks words I've been desperate to hear, so I do my best to give this new man my attention.

The man himself is definitely older, maybe sixties or so, with dark brown eyes. He's short with well-trimmed white hair. He's exactly what you'd picture a proper butler might look like, dressed conservatively in a formal waistcoat and pantsuit. If I had to describe him in one word, it would for sure be 'stuffy'.

"Oh, shit, I'm sorry. I'd have paid more attention, had I known you weren't the maids with a tray of food. Um, call me Alessandra please. Here, let me put my books away, I'd love to see the rest of the house."

"No need for that. It'll all be taken care of for you. Come, let's go." He says, as he offers me his arm to grasp.

I'm sure as shit not touching this stranger, even if he does kind of look like someone's gramps. Giving him a slightly skeptical look, I pull a robe over my silk and lace tank and pants pajama set, and then gesture for him to take the lead.

"I'd rather keep my hands to myself, if you don't mind." I say, trying to reel in my natural sass. Even doing my best impression of a sweet and innocent girl, I fail miserably. Really, it must be obvious that I just want to take his ass out with a lamp or something and run. Too bad I can guarantee that won't work out for me. For now, I have to go with the flow and work out my escape plan.

"Of course Miss." He says, a genuine sparkle in his eye, as he smiles at me. The look he gives me, tells me that he finds me entertaining, if nothing else. Maybe he can tell that I'm a fucking fake from my shit acting ability. He must expect my inner hoodrat to come out strong. Even if I say all of the right words, my resting bitch face hides nothing. I'm not exactly the sweet and sugary type of girl as it is, so let's hope I don't fuck this up.

He takes me along and we wander down two flights of stairs. I make sure to pay extra attention when we get to the bottom floor for any and all exits, as well as guards.

In a place like this, they aren't meant to be seen or heard, but they exist. I can feel the lingering presence of the unknown. It fills the air, suffocating me with their unseen presence. From an untrained eye, the manor is spectacular. If you didn't know better, you could assume this is just another show of wealth and luxury but anyone that's lived in the shadows of darkness as long as I have could sense the overwhelming danger that's stifling the air in the mansion.

"We'll start down at the bottom and work our way back to the top. You'll have noticed that there are fewer doors on the third floor and that is simply due to it being the residential space for you and the master of the estate. If you're lucky, you may even meet him today. He's been locked up there in his office for days working. I'd be curious to know if your presence is enough to pull him from his work-space." The old man says with a hopeful look in his eye. There's something there that tells me that he genuinely cares for whoever this masked man is.

Me on the other hand, I'd rather not deal with the guy today. I don't think I'm ready to face whatever monster has brought me here. I'd like to build my strength back up so I can fight him if need be.

Shivers race down my spine at the thoughts that take me back to the strange feelings from when he took care of me in my cell. Trying to suppress the shudder that's running through me, I pull my robe around me tighter, suddenly feeling too exposed. I wish I had jeans and a t-shirt available. What I wouldn't do for a pair of boots, or even sneakers.

Admittedly, I'm in a much better situation than I imagine most would find themselves in during captivity. Much worse happens every day, I know that. I've seen it with my own eyes. I really am a selfish dickhead to think I'm anywhere near on the level of others who get kidnapped. Sure, I've been stripped of my family and friends, my belongings and my freedom. I'm told I'll be forced to marry a man I do not know and do not want. But I'm alive and well. There's always a chance that I can escape. I'm strong enough to deal with what's being thrown my way.

The worst of it is that my pride has taken a hit. More than that, my entire existence is now meant to rely on a man to take care of me and tell me the who's, the what's, the when's and the where's of my life. My self-reliance has been taken in an attempt to strip me of my autonomous personality. To tame me and mold me into what is expected of me for the rest of my life.

Even Matteo's stubborn, possessive ass didn't do this. He and the guys recognized my need to control my own life, and while they pushed the boundaries and stretched all my limits, they still respected who I was and worked their way into my life instead of trying to take over, which goes against everything that Matteo is. It's making me appreciate who they are that much more, knowing how much of themselves they were willing to sacrifice to be with me. Knowing how much of themselves they gave to love me, makes my resolve to find a way home stronger. I will make it home to them. I have to.

"Um, I have kind of a weird question but do you know where my things went from when I was brought here? It would be nice to have some clothes other than pajamas if I'm going to be allowed outside my room. My current attire feels... well, inappropriate to say the least. Also, I was wearing an important piece of jewelry, it means everything to my family. A necklace that I'd very much like to keep if possible. Especially if I won't be allowed to speak with my family. It's all I have left of them." I ask, putting all of my acting skills to work.

My attempt at manipulation may fall flat unless the house staff hasn't been filled in on who I really am. I might be able to get away with the shy, nice girl act, but so far I haven't gotten much out of anyone. It's worth a shot, anyway.

"No, Miss. My apologies, but I do not. The master was the one to take care of you during your first several weeks' stay on the estate. He must have your belongings with him. You'd do well not to ask him for too much regarding your past. He's not a man you'd like to see angry. You're meant to start a new life here, my dear. It's time to leave the life you led behind you. Do you understand what I'm saying?" He asks me, looking genuinely upset about the wrath of his boss, but is he worried about me or worried that I'll upset the man he clearly cares about. It also sounds a little bit like he's trying to put me in my place. Well, fuck that.

"What, will he, like, beat me or some shit? I get that you don't know me but I'm not one to put up with a man putting his hands on a female. I don't give a fuck who he is." I spit, venom coloring my words before I can realize how much of my true self I just shared with the old man.

Looking affronted, James slowly shakes his head like I've somehow disappointed him in my assumption. Uh, did he forget about the threatening way he literally just described his boss not a full minute ago? How am I the bad guy here?

"Come Miss. We've much to see and little time to do so. Dinner will be served soon and we'll need to get you back to your room before then." He conveniently avoids answering my question while pointedly reminding me that I'll be returning me to my lovely jail cell. What I said clearly pissed him off and now I'm back in trouble. Fuck.

SEVEN

ALESSANDRA

ALL IN ALL, the first two floors of the mansion here isn't all that different from my house back at home. I don't know why but I really expected some weird red room of pain type shit. The guy I -sort of- met wears a mask, sends me devil roses and obsessive love notes. It didn't seem like too far of a stretch for him to possibly have some fucked up, kinky lair or whatever. I don't know, maybe even a full-fledged stalker room full of my pictures, given that he's stalked me basically my whole life, or like a room of dead animals and things?

Honestly, in my mind it made more sense I guess. There's a few extra amenities that I'll never use and several extra guest rooms. Just beyond the property line is a private beach that spans out for miles. I'm not allowed outside but the large floor to ceiling windows show off the insane view. The manor itself is more modern in design than that of my real home, more sleek and showy. It's made up of mostly different variations of grays, black, white and chrome. My new jail cell seems to be the most feminine of all the rooms in the large house.

"As you can see, we are back on your floor. Obviously, this is your room. Across the hall from you is the master's bedroom and next door is his office. Shall I knock to see if he's available for you?" James looks to me expectantly, like answering this correctly will forgive my earlier bitchiness downstairs.

I look to my trembling hands, whether it's from anxiety or adrenaline, I don't know, so I clasp them together to avoid him seeing it as a weakness. Looking up, I square my shoulders and nod my head. I don't want to see him, but I will not cower to this fucker. I will not allow myself to feel weak or vulnerable. I'm strong and fierce. I haven't taken shit from anyone since I was a small child and I don't intend to start now.

My mental pep talk is working wonders. Psyching myself up is giving me the clarity I've needed this whole time. I always work best under pressure, but how could I have forgotten who I am so easily. All these weeks and I've been such a soft bitch. Not today, not anymore. It's time for me to take back the control.

Knock. Knock. Knock.

James rasps his knuckles solidly on the door before opening it slightly and announcing his arrival. He looks back to me and holds up one finger before shutting the door in my face.

What the hell? Why does everything around here have to be so suspicious? I mean, they've already kidnapped me for shit's sake. They have security up the ass and I have zero idea of where I am or how to leave. The secrecy might as well get thrown out the window now, since this guy assumes he'll be marrying me.

Oh, shit. I wonder if he's beastly? Maybe he wears the mask because he's ugly as hell and is afraid I'll run and hide once I see his ogre face. How could I not have thought about that before? For the longest time, I genuinely thought it was Lorenzo DeLuca but that can't be right. The guy that's been visiting me in the cellar seemed younger and his oddly familiar raspy smoker's voice had the faintest of Italian accents. Plus, his entire being exudes power.

It's one of the reasons why I was so dazed and confused in the cellar. I could almost put Matteo in his place in my mind. Matteo's father may have continued to build his 'business', using it as a front for his shady dealings, after my bisnonna sold most of her shares. It's now nothing more than a low life, underground, shady as fuck sex slavery business, but he isn't strong or powerful. He's insecure and pathetic. A weak man that wears his evil as a mask for all to see to hide the spineless, gutless piece of shit he really is. It's what makes him seem like he's a proud businessman who takes charge and doesn't take shit from anyone, but really there's a reason he went into a business that allows him to prey on those weaker and more vulnerable than anyone else. He couldn't control the mafia if he wanted to. He'd be chewed up and spit out. He may have control over women and children but he could never rule over a kingdom of powerful men.

Hearing the door creak open, I look up into the delighted face of James. His smile is so broad, it overtakes his whole face. Joy and pride light up his eyes. He's clearly happy about his little pow wow with his boss- err- master? Yuck, even thinking that sounds like the beginning to a bad porno. No thanks, we'll go with his boss.

"The master of the house will see you now, miss Alessandra." He smiles.

I'm going to have to talk to him about this master shit. It's giving me all the bad vibes. If I get stuck here, married to this guy for real, would that make me the mistress of the house? Ugh, no. Bad thoughts, can we just not? I have goosebumps from how bad that makes me feel all over.

Clearing my mind, I walk into the office, but refuse to look anywhere except the old butlers face yet. I don't owe this guy my respect.

"Thank you James, I can take things from here." I say to the old man, feeling the need for some privacy to face off with big bad.

"Of course, Miss. Call for me when you're ready for an escort back to your sleeping quarters. Unless, of course, you find yourself preoccupied." He gives me a knowing smirk.

Uh, what? My eyes widen slightly at the insinuation. My body locking up tight and my gaze narrows as I glare at him while he leaves me alone with the masked man in the office. Although, when I finally look his way, his desk chair is turned away from me at the moment and I have no idea if he's actually wearing his mask right now.

"So, are you ever going to show me your face or-"

"Drink?" He cuts me off, rasping his question at me in that smokey baritone voice of his, standing up abruptly and moving to the drink cart in the back corner of his spacious office.

"Water if you have it, otherwise, no." I say, knowing having a drink is likely a bad idea.

He shrugs a shoulder in response and gets to work pouring drinks. I take the time to look him over from behind, both nervous and anxious to finally see his face when he turns around. He wore a fitted dark gray suit today and from the looks of things, he wears it well. His suit jacket is slung carelessly over the back of the rich, dark leather chair at his desk. His crisp black button up shirt has the sleeves rolled up to his forearms, showcasing the crazy number of tattoos that cover his arms. He has a strong build, his back muscles visible against the tight dress shirt that is tucked into equally fitted, black suit pants. I'm not gonna lie, that ass is fine.

I still hate him, but I can admit when someone is attractive. His hair looks to be on the longer side. Longest on the top and slicked back out of his face. I can't quite tell but if I had to guess, I'd assume it's styled similar to that of a greaser back in the day. I don't have a clear view of his face and he's made sure to dim the lights a bit before I came in here but I think there's a hint of stubble along his jaw. Just thinking about how attractive he might be, makes me think of my handsome guys back home. I will not cry again but fuck if I don't miss them with every breath I take.

Closing me eyes, I breathe in... two... three... four. I breathe out... two... three... four.

I can smell him, before I feel his presence. His clean soap scent, overwhelming my senses. He's right up in my space now and I know that I need to open my eyes and face the monster that's hidden in the shadows all these years. I give myself one extra moment before I slowly open my eyes to his broad chest.

I look downward to the movement of him handing me a glass of ice cold water, reaching out to take it. Once I have the glass in my hands, I slowly move my eyes up the length of his body, the body that was pressed up against me not that long ago. The electrically charged air swirls around us as I look at his hands, his arms, his chest and neck.

Noticing that he has one long stemmed black rose tattooed to the right side of his neck. His ears are gauged, not too big, just enough to give him a little more edge. I look at his defined, stubbled jaw and thick, full lips. I look at his strong, straight nose that's pierced on both sides with two small diamond studs. But it's when I make my eyes meet his that I can't hold back the gasp that falls from my lips or the glass that falls from my hand.

"Oh. My. God..."

I speak the words so softly; I have no idea if they made their way into the universe. A stray tear leaks from my eye without permission as I look up into the eyes that are as familiar to me as my own. Those that mirror the eyes of the man I love.

"Ciao, mi amore." He allows the intimate low rasp of his voice to caress me like a long lost lover, overwhelming every one of my senses.

"Oh, fuck..." It escapes before I can stop it and then I pass out into the arms of this familiar stranger.

EIGHT

ALESSANDRA

OPENING my eyes I find myself looking deep into the sparkling emerald gaze that I could spend the rest of my life peering into. He's watching me sleep, just like he used to. I'd often times wake up to Matteo, Cohen or Noah just blissfully watching over me as I slept, sometimes softly grazing my arms, shoulders, neck or face, like they couldn't help themselves. Their need to touch me overwhelming them so much that it was worth the risk of pulling me from my peaceful sleep.

"'Teo... God, I've missed you." I feel tears leaking out of my eyes when I reach my hand up to touch his stubbled jaw. He normally keeps his face a little more clean cut but the new beard growth looks disarmingly good on him.

"Don't cry baby. I'm here." He rasps, wiping the slow trickle of tears from my face.

"The guys will be here soon as well, but do you know what I want to do to you in the meantime?" He asks, smirking sinfully like the dark devil he is.

He moves down the length of my body, taking my panties and

pants with him, drawing out small whimpers from me thanks to the little touches he draws from his fingers.

"God, I've missed you." He rasps.

He builds every ounce of anticipation he can and It's working because every inch of me feels like a trail of fire licks across each sliver of skin he uncovers. When he gets down to my thighs, he pushes them open as wide as he can, licking me from bottom to top, before placing a kiss right on my clit. He gives no other warning before he devours me.

Without wasting anymore time, he dives his face into my pussy, eating me like I'm his last meal. His teasing on my clit only serves to drive my desire for him higher. My vision becomes hazy and I feel like I'm losing all control as I thrust my fingers into his hair and shove his face further into my pussy, while he fucks me proper with his tongue. My back bows off of the bed as I breathily moan his name.

"Matteo, please!" I beg.

Vigorously, he slides a finger into me and, holy shit does that feel good. So, so, so fucking good, I'm damn near explosive. I can feel myself coating his finger as he slides a second one into me, I'm so wet it slides in easily, stretching me out and causing him to groan loudly. Pumping in and out of me, he curls his fingers and hits my g-spot just as he gently bites my clit. Oh. My...

"Yeessss!" I scream, as he continues to pump his fingers in and out of me relentlessly, bringing on the commanding force of a second orgasm before my body has even finished convulsing from the first. I need him to stop. I need him to come with me.

"C'mon love, give me all of you. Don't make me wait anymore. I need you, 'Teo please. I need you to fuck me." I beg him.

I've missed him too much; I've been without him too long. I don't want to wait anymore. I'd prefer all of the guys be here but I'm lost in a sex fog and I know they'll take care of me when they get here.

"Fuck. But you taste too sweet. I could do this all day." He groans, taking one last lick of my dripping pussy, circling my clit and causing me to shiver with pleasure, before he nips at it and moves back up the length of my body. There's zero hesitation when his face meets mine

and he moves in for a rough kiss that flips my world upside down. It's so passionate, almost violent.

He's missed me too. Allowing me to taste myself on his lips, he tangles his tongue with mine, showing me all of his dominance in that one kiss and then he pushes himself inside of me and I fall apart. I'm completely unable to stop myself from coming after already being on the brink of orgasm thanks to the way he worked me up so well with his magical tongue and fingers.

"Oh, fuck. Don't move yet baby. Your cunt is gripping me so tight; I could come already. Don't make me embarrass myself." He huffs out a weird mix between a groan and a laugh in that sexy raspy growl of his.

And then, he moves.

He. Fucking. Moves.

Sliding in and out of my wet heat, building up a pressure deep inside me I didn't know existed. It's so deep and so powerful. It started out as a small tingle, but it's quickly grown and became more and more extreme. It's everything. Seriously, I hope he never stops doing exactly this. Each powerful thrust brings me back to the edge of sweet oblivion and I just want to stay there, suspended in an orgasmic daze.

Just when I think I can't take anymore hanging on the precipice of my orgasm, he moves his hand down and pinches one of my nipples, sending a whole new ripple of pleasure through me, straight to my clit and I come all over him. The pleasure is so intense, it radiates throughout my entire body.

"Shit. Shit. Shit. 'Teo. Oh, fuck!" I scream, past the point of giving a fuck over how loud I might be.

"Yes, baby. Come all over my cock. Fucking hell, keep that death grip on my dick." He roars, coming deep inside me.

"Damn woman, you're going to ruin me." He teases but the look in his eye is deadly serious.

He looks at me like I'm everything right in his world. His love for me is pouring from every ounce of who he is.

"I love you Alessandra. You'll always be with me, trust in that.

Like you said, 'There will never be a time when my heart can't find yours.'" He whispers as he rolls me over and pulls me into him, my back to his front. Nuzzling my neck, he presses a long kiss just behind my ear.

"Go back to sleep beautiful girl." He rumbles, just before my eyes close and sleep consumes me.

I wake up wet and moaning, needy and desperate for the warmth of my boys' love and affection. I'm turned on and I'm hot all over, wrapped up in a cocoon of soft blankets with a hard body pressed up against mine. My body is being held down by the weight of a strong arm and I feel an intimidatingly large, thick dick nestled into the crack of my ass. Still lost in the haze of my dream, my body involuntarily pushes back against it in small gyrating motions and the arm pulls me closer. A long muscular leg pushes in between my thighs, allowing their dick the space it needs to be pushed into me further.

Subtly, I continue to grind on his cock, making me vaguely aware of the fact that I've been stripped down to just a t-shirt. Not even a bra or panties are on me, so the only thing between me and the monster dick I'm riding is the thin layer of fabric from boxer briefs. A large hand lifts the hem of my shirt, trailing slowly up the course of my body to graze the underneath side of my breasts, before pinching my left nipple and following the trail it made back down my body, caressing my skin from hip bone to hip bone. I feel plump, full lips move sensually along my neck, and every sensation suddenly becomes heightened as I become desperate with desire, causing me to moan at the contact. It's been too long since I've had an orgasm that wasn't dream induced. I'm so lost in the dreamy haze of orgasmic wonder that I almost don't register it when he moans.

My brain too slowly recognizes that it isn't a moan of Cohen,

Noah or Matteo and my body locks up just as his hand moves further down, finding my pussy wet and wanting. I'm stuck where I am and part of me is so desperate for the feel of his touch, wishing desperately that my dream wasn't really a dream. But if it wasn't then the arm holding me down and the moaning voice is that of the familiar stranger. *His* perfect look alike. The only differences being the disarming tattoos and piercings, that shouldn't be as hot as they are.

That alone should have me pushing the guy away but something keeps me there, something other than his physical presence. The energy surrounding me is raw and heated, but somehow peaceful, calming even. Not the usual menacing vibes I get from the masked man, but also not the overly confident understanding of my body that my boys have, now that I'm alert enough to pay attention. He's more tentative with his touches, perfectly content to take his time while learning the landscape of my body. He swirls his fingers around my clit, and my body relaxes some just before he plunges one, then two fingers inside of me. My pussy contracts without my permission, tightening around his fingers and I feel my breathing accelerate while my body succumbs to the much needed orgasm as it washes over my body. I've been so tightly wound that nothing could've prevented my body from that release even though I know how wrong it is.

I move to roll my body over to face whoever is in my bed but once again, I'm held in place, which causes me to start inwardly panicking. Things have already gone way too far!

"What the fuck?" I growl, allowing my annoyance to surface and be vocalized.

Bringing me hands up, I try to push his heavy arms off of me and wiggle my body to try and escape his firm hold on me.

"Don't mi amore. I want to spend just another moment with you wrapped up in my arms before you freak out on me for touching you." He rasps in a sleepy smokers voice that sends tingles all throughout my body. Once again convincing me that I may have developed some form of Stockholm syndrome, because it brings me so much peace.

I stop wiggling all over and listen to the oddly calming sound of his voice. I'm really going to need my body to catch up to my brain here, I don't need to be attracted to this guy, but I feel connected to him in a way that I can't even begin to explain. I'm angry, true. I'm also becoming invested in figuring out why his presence affects me so deeply.

Again, I move to roll over and this time he allows it. I don't freak out like I know I should - like he assumes I will. In fact, typically I'd be fighting, scratching and clawing my way out of a situation like this, but I'll admit that I'm fascinated.

Reaching my hand up to touch him, I move some of his longer hair off of his forehead and trace my fingernail gently down his face, touching every feature he has. My wide eyed gaze takes in the same full, pout and strong jaw, although with a lot more stubble than I'm used to. The same straight nose and alluring eyes. I allow myself to really look at this unknown man and get the overwhelming sense that I know him. And not just in the sense that he's a carbon copy of *him*. It feels like he's been mine my whole life and somehow I missed it or ignored it maybe. All of the sickness and fear brought on by his weird love notes disappear.

Something about the look in his eyes makes me confident that he didn't do any of it to be a creepy freak of nature. There's more to the story and I need to figure out what's happening. How could I feel so strongly about a stranger, especially when my heart already belongs to three other men?

"Who are you?" I whisper, afraid of what the answer might actually be. Confusion coloring my tone.

He allows me to keep tracing lines along his face, and down his neck as he answers.

"My name is Lorenzo DeLuca Junior."

NINE

MY NAME IS LORENZO DELUCA JUNIOR…

Those are the words that really just came out of his mouth. He's watching me closely, gauging my reaction. I imagine he's seeing a healthy amount of shock staring back at him while I try to piece together what little information I have.

"Wait… What?" My brain finally computes enough that I can almost form real words. I must look and sound like a moron.

"Legally I'm Lorenza DeLuca Junior, but I'm publicly known as Ren Gavino. I'm an underboss to the Gavino family, the Italian mafia of the East coast. I am the son of Arianna Gavino and Lorenzo DeLuca, also I am the eldest twin to Matteo DeLuca." He says, calmly like he's reciting the fucking alphabet and not dropping nuclear fact bombs on my brain.

"What the actual fuck is happening right now?" I ask myself quietly. My brain is trying to process the information, but everything seems to be bypassing my brain, refusing to take in all of the information at once, as I gradually digest his words. My body jerks back involuntarily in self-preservation, causing him to hold me tighter.

"I am not a good guy, Quinn. I know this. Admittedly, this is all a lot to take in, but there's more to our story than you know. To be perfectly honest, I am un bastardo egoista - a selfish bastard, and I won't ever let you go. I need you to understand that mia bella. I need you to understand before I tell you anything else." His faint accent becomes a bit more pronounced when he's passionate about something and it would be hot if I weren't starting to feel pushed into a corner and left defenseless.

I try to push off of him, needing space to process all the shit he just dropped on me and wrap my brain around it, but he pulls me closer.

"Don't push me away Quinn. I can answer all of your questions but don't push me away, per favore." he asks.

"You called me Quinn." It isn't a question but a statement - a realization. I move my face, to angle myself to properly look into his eyes as he speaks, looking for as much truth as possible.

"Si, I'm only six months older than you and when you were promised to me, we weren't even born yet. We were still just toddlers when we met for the first time. I couldn't pronounce Alessandra so I called you Quinn whenever we were allowed to see each other. You probably don't remember me but we were best friends, completely inseparable, until we were about five years old and then I had to start working with private tutors and mio nonno, and you had to be placed with Lauren to keep you hidden from your famiglia. If Alessandro Salvatore had known you were with us at our estate, there would've been an all-out war." His gaze tracks mine, like he knows I'm trying to peer into his dark soul.

Holy shit. This is more complicated than I could've ever imagined.

"Does Matteo know you exist?" I ask, suddenly feeling slightly betrayed that 'Teo would keep something like this from me.

"No. We were separated at birth. I went with mia madre and he went with nostro padre - our father. The deal was that Lorenzo would be allowed to keep and raise my brother if he gave Raffaele Gavino something in return. Lorenzo gave you up to the Gavino family to ensure he'd have a son to pass on his legacy to. I was the oldest so it made sense that I would be the one to go to the Gavino family. It ensured that the original contracts between the Salvatore's and the Bianchi/DeLuca families were fulfilled for Lorenzo but didn't give him any real power.

"By birth you are a descendant of the Salvatore's on your great grandfather's side and Bianchi on your great grandmother's side. The contract states that a female descendant must go forth to marry a DeLuca to create equal power within their business by creating one bloodline. Your great grandparents could only conceive your grandfather and things didn't work out with your mother. When it was known that you were a female, Lorenzo worked out a plan. In doing so, I had to be named after my piece of shit father to keep the paperwork legitimate. Once our past is settled and all of the original deals have been concluded, I can legally change everything to the Gavino name." He looks to me to see if I'm still listening.

There's no doubt about it, I'm locked in for story time. So many pieces to the puzzle are finally coming together. He reaches out and pushes some stray hair from my face before continuing.

"When Lorenzo first realized that he hadn't won the heart of your mother, he had slept with my momma out of spite and resentment, only to try and gain Cecelia's favor again and in doing so breaking the heart of my mom. It was stupid on his part to screw over one mafia princess to gain favor of another. In the end, neither wanted him and he royally pissed off mio nonno, Raffaele. Several months later when it came out that your mother had already conceived you, Lorenzo came up with the plans to keep what little power he had and to create peace with the Gavino family. No one knew he had been with mia madre so he told everyone that he'd impregnated a maid, who eventually became known as Matteo's mom publicly.

"Once we were born, Matteo stayed in California and my momma brought me back to New York to raise me. Rumor has it that he blackmailed one of his maids into going along with the story. He wanted no one to know the truth. He wanted Matteo to grow up and rule the West coast under your grandfather and has been raising him as the only known DeLuca heir. Meanwhile, I'm known as a Gavino publicly and legally a DeLuca." He finishes his story and I think I'm stuck in a state of shock because even at the worst of times, I've been all sass and backtalk but I've got nothing.

My heart is broken for these boys and their horrifying upbringings. I hate Lorenzo DeLuca in a way that I never thought possible. He's such a despicable human being. No words will form in my mouth. I just stare at this guy, wrapped up in him intimately despite not knowing him, letting him tell me his truth. Our truth, I guess. It's ugly and fucked up in the highest order but that's the life we lead.

"Lorenzo told Matteo I was promised to him though. Even my nonno said that if I wanted him, it was the natural course of things in our world. They were all renegotiating the contracts so that I could technically marry into all of the surrounding families for Matteo, Noah and Cohen. It was ideal to make all of the surrounding territories to the West coast more cohesive. Cohen and Noah have incredibly powerful families in their own right." I say quietly. More thinking out loud than anything else.

"He was probably saving face once everything went to shit in Chicago. Lauren died when we were all handling business overseas and somehow there was a miscommunication on who was supposed to be your caseworker. It was a mess and several people died because I lost you. I already told you, I am not one to fuck over or piss off. I am the youngest East coast underboss for a reason and it's not because of who my grandfather is. I'm known best for my cruelty and efficiency in killing those who cross me or make an enemy of the Gavino famiglia. And sometimes those who haven't yet." He says, smirking. He's clearly proud of that fact. My body lets out an involuntary shudder in response, both in fear and because it's kind of a turn on.

"If you're my age, how are you not in school. How are you already running things?" I ask, needing as much information as possible.

"I was privately tutored from a young age, I surpassed all of my high school courses by the time I was fifteen. I have mostly spent the last couple of years working under Raffaele Gavino, la Don of the Eastern territories. I was raised between the Gavino Estates in New York and a small coastal town in Italy, Portofino, under my bisnonno's tutelage. Whenever I was in the states, I made sure to check in on you personally and when I couldn't be here, I made sure la famiglia's guys had eyes on you. I know your life wasn't great growing up, but I wasn't technically allowed to step in until you were eighteen. I swear I've been in your life protecting you when I could though. Honestly, my grandfather will be furious to know that I've already taken you back before it's time. I'll need you to prepare yourself for his cruelty. I know you're strong, but he is vicious.

"I had to put much faith in nothing bad happening to you because no one wanted to go against my grandfather - and then later myself, if anything did happen to you during the times that I was away. I wasn't joking when I said that I've loved you for years mia bella, I've loved you my whole life. You've always been mine." He whispers the last part, as though he's afraid he'll lose me now that he finally has me within his grasp, literally.

Suddenly, I feel like I can't breathe. Everything is hitting me at once and I'm starting to feel a rising panic within me. I need to work all of this out in my mind so I can calm down and come up with a resolution. I can't give up my boys. I love them too much to let them go. I have power too, I am Alessandra fucking Salvatore for fucks' sake, I can handle this. Looking up at the handsome stranger before me, I recognize the weird energy between us for what it is. I've been ignoring it all this time, it's a knowingness, a closeness that can't be denied. I've been feeling as though I've known him all my life, and I guess I have, in a way. It reminds me of the connection I feel to the guys and my heart feels like it's crumbling to pieces.

I drop my gaze from his, and shove away from him as much as he'll let me.

"Ren, I need a little space. This is a lot of information and my immediate reaction is to fight or run, neither of which will do me any good right now. You may have been watching me or protecting me or whatever all this time, but I don't know you. Not really. And to be perfectly honest, it's not fair to you that I'm in love with three other people when you clearly see our life planned out differently." I finally look back to him.

I'm not saying it to be mean or cruel, but because honesty is important to me and I think going forward it will get me farther than my original plan of playing along until I can get free. He looks equally hurt and furious, with the thinning of his lips and the narrowing of his eyes. I can feel his hands forming fists behind my back.

"Hey, I'm not saying anything to purposefully make you upset. I just feel like we have a lot of history to work through and if you really want to be with me, like you've been saying, then it's best to be honest with each other. My love for Noah, Cohen and Matteo isn't diminishing or going away. They're a part of me as much as you are. I'm sorry that it angers you, but I'm not sorry that it's my truth. If you want my heart, you need to recognize that you aren't the only one who will take up residence there. My soul will always find a way to theirs and you'll need to come to terms with that.

"The possessiveness in you runs deep in your brother as well, but you'll need to learn quick just like he did that I don't play that game. I'm my own person and just as much as you don't want me to push you, you'll need to respect the fact that I'm a force to be reckoned with, just like you. I'm new to the mafia life but I've picked it up real quick and now I have a job to do, just the same as you. Know it, trust it and fucking respect it because it's not changing. You don't get to kidnap me and act like a crazy stalker every time you don't get your way. You don't even have to. If you want my attention, it's yours. Just give me time to get to know you. Let me talk to my family so they know that I'm alive and doing ok. I can agree to give us some time but you'll need to lessen the restraints a bit. As far as I'm concerned, the only bad guy here is your father. Can you trust me?" I ask, knowing that I've crossed so many of his lines.

This is a guy used to being in charge and controlling everything. A young man, destined to live a dangerous and violent life so his need to take over is ingrained deeply into him, just as it is my other three, but he needs to know that I can help. I can be his counterpart without him losing his reign over everything. I won't, however, give up on the other three men in my life, nor will I lose the little family I have left. I will make Lorenzo pay one day for his recklessness and selfishness. He doesn't get to hurt everyone and climb to the top of the food chain by association.

"I don't know what to say to that. I want to give you the fucking world Quinn but I don't think I can share you. I'm a possessive asshole on a good day, you already know this. It's destroying me to know that you've given your heart to not just one, but three other guys. This is an entirely unorthodox situation you've created. What you're asking of me is unheard of in our world. Even if I could look past my own desires, I don't know how to give it to you because it's simply not how things are done. I need you, and not in some trivial way. Yes, my body craves you, my mind desires you, but my heart and soul belong to you. I can't wait any longer to have you by my side and to be completely honest, I don't want to share you. There's never been a situation like this before within la famiglia. Women aren't leaders. If they are promised to a man, they are not to stray from that man without risking their life in the process. They get no say in the matter, they are to do what they're told. I'm scared for you because of that, but also for what's to come if I can find it within myself to look past my own selfish needs and give you what you want. I don't even know if I can." He tells me.

It's not what I want to hear, but it's the truth. It's his truth. I'm angry about it but I'm stuck for now. It's not uncommon knowledge that women have a place in the life of the mafia and it's an ugly place at that. They are to be seen and not heard. They tend to be trophies or toys.

Wives have some level of respect, but they are kept in the dark more often than not. I am the opposite. I'm being groomed to take over the underworld, whether on my own or with my men at my side, but it's supposed to be my choice. The East coast territories clearly aren't as progressive as the West coast. I'll work this out one way or another though.

"I get it, really I do, but I'm not going to be locked up here like your little princess in the tall tower. If nothing else, I'd like my gun, knife and necklace back and to call my family. They don't deserve to be put through this again by you and your family. I'll also need to inform them that there's to be a hit on Lorenzo. His business is to be dismantled and made legitimate so that I can take back what originally belonged to my family. If I'm what's left of the Bianchi bloodline, it's rightfully mine anyway. Or ours, I guess since you and 'Teo are his descendants. Either way, he's done ruining people's lives and I'm going to see to it that he no longer can." I turn a glare on him to let him know that I mean it.

I've been nice because I'm still learning to understand my feelings and because I'm not stupid enough to think I have much control right now, but that doesn't mean I'll lay down and be a doormat. I know what's expected of women in the mafia families traditionally and that shit won't work for me.

"Let's get some more rest for now, it's three in the morning and I'd like to keep you in my arms for a while longer if you'll let me. We can talk through all of this in the morning. For now, let yourself process the info I've given you and get some more sleep." He says as he pulls me back into him and down onto the mattress.

If there's anything I've learned from falling for my boys, it's that it's better to allow my feelings to guide me instead of my instinct to push everyone away and keep them at arm's length. I'm not going to fight him off... at least not *yet*, but things are about to change. The East coast isn't ready for me to be back, that much I know.

TEN

ALESSANDRA

BREAKFAST IS DELICIOUS. Waffles with strawberries and whipped cream. Yes please. All day, every freaking day. It's my meal of choice. Ren even thought ahead to make sure he's well stocked up on my favorite energy drink. When I saw that tall black can with its shiny golden star, I almost cried from happiness. That shit's my life essence, I swear.

I was allowed to eat in the dining hall with Ren instead of being locked away in my room again. He didn't say a whole lot but I think he's feeling some of the hostility I feel about being locked up in this gilded cage. Giving me time to sleep on all of the information back-fired a bit because now I'm more angry than before.

This guy doesn't actually know me. He thinks he does, but how can he say he's in love with me when the last time we spent any real time together, we were barely potty trained. Really, he's just been taught to think he loves me through familial obligation. Maybe it's the pessimist in me, but this isn't how falling in love works. Hell, this isn't how life works. If I didn't know firsthand what it means to fall in love, I'd be a lot more defensive right now, that much I do know. If nothing else, I'm curious to see what these intense feelings lead to.

Ren and I have a strong connection. I feel it deep in my bones but that doesn't mean we should get married and make babies or anything. Also, fuck him for thinking he can tell me what to do. I think it's time we find a gym because I'm ready to kick his ass for assuming I'd just drop my whole life without a fight.

"Hey, you got a gym in this mausoleum?" I ask, ready to throw the fuck down. My body is desperate for a real physical beatdown. I need to work out until I'm worn out. It's how I process shit. I haven't fought anyone in who knows how long and I'm going crazy.

"Yes, of course. It's in the basement. I have everything you'll need for any kind of training you choose to do. I made sure to redesign the room for you when I noticed you were a natural fighter. We can spar if you'd like." He grins at me, a knowing smile on his handsome face.

"Hell. Yes. Let's go." I say, all but running towards the stairs. I stop abruptly when I realize I only have lingerie and pj's, and it causes Ren to slam into me. His hands grab ahold of my hips to steady the both of us, but it ends up being more of a bump and grind type situation.

"If you wanted my hands on you, all you had to do is say so." He growls out. His hips shifting so that I feel his forming hard on. I pull away from him before he takes things further.

"Uh, no perv. I don't have any clothes to work out in. All you've given me so far is sexy underwear and nightgowns. Is that, like, a fetish or something?" I ask sarcastically.

"Yeah, actually it is. Problem?" He deadpans, before giving me a megawatt smile that lets me know he's joking. It's hard to be mad at him when he looks so much like my 'Teo. I have to start paying attention to his mannerisms more so I can differentiate them in my mind. You'd think the tattoos and piercings would do it, but it doesn't detract from how much he looks like his twin. I won't be doing anyone any favors by allowing my brain to make them the same person. But even his subtle dry humor is similar and it does something weird to my heartstrings.

"There's actually workout gear in the gym for you and you have clothes in my closet. I never had them moved over because... Well, I guess I'm still holding out hope that you'll make the decision on your own to become mine. You were originally supposed to move directly into our room, but I decided to give you your own space to help you adjust instead. It feels like a cliché mafia movie move to force your hand, but if you can't come to terms with this life on your own, eventually Raffaele will step in. I've done everything I can to keep him out of our business so far." He tells me. His hands are still on my hips, but he's unable to look me in the eye, as if he's embarrassed that his grandfather is stuck in some misogynistic old way of thinking.

"Let's just go work out and we'll talk about all this shit later. I need to burn some energy off before I can come at everything you've told me with a clear head." I say, and then take off in a sprint to the basement, excited to put something other than jammies on.

"Ho-ly crap." I'm a bit stunned at the sheer size of the gym itself. It's equipped with everything my dark little fighter heart could ever want and I'm practically drooling. Moving over to a row of lockers I see that there are, in fact, gym clothes for me. There are spandex shorts and leggings, sports bras, crop tops, long and short sleeve t-shirts, socks and what looks to be every pair of running shoes ever made. There is tape and boxing gloves and headgear...

This is the first time since being here that I genuinely feel happy and in my element. I was horny, curious and caught off guard in the early morning hours and I allowed myself to be more open to Ren than I normally would have, but now I need to keep him at a slight distance until I can figure out why he causes me to have such a visceral reaction to him, other than being the tattooed version of his sexy as sin brother.

There's something about him that, even before I knew who he was, made my heart beat wildly in my chest. It could be anything, frustration, confusion or excitement. Whatever it is, I'm keeping it in check until I get to know him.

I turn my gaze to his and find him watching me intently. I could be bold and change here in front of him but that would likely be me pushing my luck. Especially since I'm so attracted to him, it would blur the lines I'm trying to set and I don't want to lead him on. So, I grab some clothes and look for a bathroom to change in. When I don't see one I know I'm going to have to ask where I can change.

"Is there a bathroom or somewhere I can put these clothes on, or is the *master* of the house going to demand his little whore undresses in front of him?" I snark, knowing I'm being a bitch but, hey, it's my go to defense mechanism. I'm struggling to define a line between right and wrong in a place that is clearly wrong. It was clearly the wrong choice because he covers the distance between us in an instant and is all up in my face. Any normal girl would be terrified of this hulking man beast all up in their shit with his scowl aimed directly at them. Good thing I sure as shit ain't normal.

Boxing me in against the lockers, he brings his arms up and places his hands on either side of me and brings his mouth close to my ear. He's practically nuzzling my neck before he speaks.

"Quinn, there are very few rules I will ever have between us when we are alone but hear me when I tell you this because I'll only say it this one... Fucking... Time. You will not demean our relationship or disrespect what I feel for you. I am fully aware that you are upset and confused right now and I'm willing to give you time and be patient with you while we navigate through this together. If you are angry take it out on me in this room or in our bed. If you need to speak your mind, you tell me whatever it is you need to say, but do not, and I mean this, do fucking not make a mockery of who you are to me. This is not a joke. You are my life and will at some point be my wife. Honor that." He commands, his naturally quiet, rough voice somehow feels booming and powerful against my skin. It reverberates through the empty cavity in my chest. His entire being is one of power and demands a level of respect I've only seen in a few other men.

With that he takes a small nip at my ear, then shifts to grab his own work out clothing from a shelf and turns away from me to change, leaving me in awe and simultaneously giving me the privacy

I was looking for. I keep my eye on him to make sure he doesn't peek at me but in the back of my mind I somehow know he won't. This guy genuinely respects me. I know he's seen all of me since he obviously was the one to take care of me after he fucking drugged me and I was unconscious, but there's something about how respectful he is about my need for privacy and personal space that both infuriates me and makes my heart swell at his thoughtfulness. My righteous indignation over my mistreatment to get me here is still simmering in the pot of my emotions and I'll let that out when we hit the mats.

When Ren finally turns around my teenage hormone fueled brain gets the better of me for a moment and I damn near have to pick my jaw up off the floor. The dude is stacked. Muscles on muscles and so many of them are covered in remarkable artwork. His tattoo artist is a good one. He's wearing basketball shorts and a cut off tank that has arm holes so massive, he's basically not wearing a shirt. I can see that he has his nipples pierced and immediately my brain conjures up images of other areas he may have pierced as well.

"You wanna fight or stare at my dick all day?" Grinning like the cat who got the freaking canary, he walks back to me and places his hands back on my hips - a place he seems to really love. It's enough to snap me out of the daydream I found myself in. I hadn't realized that I was actually staring at the star of my short lived fantasy.

What the fuck is *wrong* with me? Teenage hormones suck balls. You'd think I'd have learned this with my guys, but it's like I'm making up for lost time or some shit and I'm living in a constant state of horny bitch. Didn't want to date when everyone else around me started because fuck guys. Except now I want *four* of them for keeps? Nah, my shit's all messed up. I need a shrink. I thought I was crazy for wanting three dudes at once. Ugh, I'm a hot mess.

"Shut up!" I shove him away and move to the mats to try and hide the flush on my cheeks. Whether it's from being turned on or embarrassment at being caught, maybe both, I'm not sure, but my face feels really hot. Embarrassment isn't really my style so I throw a little sass at him to gain my sense of self back a little.

"You gonna fight me or nah? I'd understand if you were afraid of me. Most men can't handle what I've got." I smirk, while taping up my hands, not bothering to look at him.

He walks over to me and tips my chin up so my eyes meet his own, they sparkle with mischief as he bends down and grazes his lips across my own.

"I can handle you, mi amore, don't you worry about that." He says, just before his nips at my lips playfully and then turns to tape up his own hands.

What is this universe that I've found myself in? Nothing makes sense here, including my own reaction to this fascinating boy. If any other random ass guy tried that, they'd already have had their asses handed to them - or be dead. Is it a fetish thing? Am I attracted to men of power? Am I attracted to killers? I think I need to see that shrink before I make any other life altering decisions. For now, I'm going to box this giant man beast and work all of my hormonal horniness out of my system and regain some god damn clarity.

I start stretching and shaking out my arms and bouncing on the balls of my feet. I've kept up with some basic floor workouts but that's nothing compared to what I can do in this gym. Moving over to a speed bag I start hitting it slow, developing my rhythm before picking up speed to work on my coordination and endurance. I hear music come on overhead, it sounds like *Inside Out* by Conor Matthews, but I'm too zoned in on the bag to take much notice. I throw a few extra elbows in there just to see if I can still keep up the rhythm I've got going on and when I feel like I've gotten a good handle on it, I switch up my rhythm and move even faster to improve my timing.

ELEVEN

ALESSANDRA

I'M SO focused on my workout, I don't even realize when Ren moves in on me. He flips me around to face him and I'm so startled, I bring my fist around, swinging for his face on instinct. He takes a step back to dodge my move, which only makes me want to go harder. He holds his hands up like he's guarding his face and gives me a come on motion so I move in on him throwing all my best moves at him, but he's fast, faster than Noah even. I don't give up though. I use my anger towards everything happening in my life to go on the offense and attack with the best of my ability.

Finally I land a kidney punch and it barely phases him, but it does get him to fight back. It's not long before I've gotten a few good face shots in and I'm starting to feel a lot better. The smacking sounds coming from each hit, the grunts from every elbow or kick we throw, the crack of knuckles as we slam our fist into each other is just another high I get from my own warped version of therapy. I'm going to feel it all later, but I'm proud to say I'm giving as good as I'm getting and I'm so fucking ecstatic that he's not treating me like I'm a girl. I'm not some little bitch and he's showing me respect by fighting back.

Before I know it, though, I end up working defensively countering his attacks. Jab, jab, uppercut. None of it works. Every ounce of space I put between us; he adjusts so I can't find any breathing room. He's coming at me too hard and too fast for me to counter with enough force to win this match. I'm learning a lot though, both about him and myself. He's a fucking monster in the ring. I pity anyone fighting him for real.

Next thing I know I'm being brought down with a swift swipe of his legs, bringing mine out from under me. I go down hard with my head bouncing off the mat and I'm surprised to find that I'm actually turned on by him not taking it easy on me. I push him up with my arms and use my lower body strength to flip over so our roles are reversed and I'm on top of him. I bring my arms up to pin his to the mat in hopes that he'll cave and tap out. It's been too long and I'm getting worn out and I haven't even done any circuit training yet.

When I push down on his arms, my face aligns with his and we are both breathing hard. My core is rubbing against his lower abs and instinctively my legs tighten against his hips. Every movement is beginning to feel more erotic than violent, which only becomes more intense when the song changes to *As You Are* by The Weeknd. We are both breathing hard and our bodies are so close, I can feel his heartbeat start to increase to a rapid pace. At this point I can't tell if my breathing is labored because of the intense workout or because of Ren.

I release his hold and move to sit up but he comes up with me and I end up in his lap, with my legs wrapped around him. Our noses are touching because of how quickly he moved with my motions and before I know what's happening, Ren's hands are tangled in the hair at the nape of my neck and he's pushing our lips together with unrestrained force. He's clearly been holding himself back up until this point because this kiss makes my body feel like it's been doused in gasoline and the match lit.

Knowing that I can cause him to lose control fills me with the most intoxicating energy. I can feel his need straining against his shorts and my brain says to back off and run for safe ground, but my body, the needy bitch she is, grinds down hard on him, moaning and allowing him full access to my mouth. He swirls his tongue against mine and I moan louder. It feels like my whole body is being hit with tiny electric charges and my body starts tingling as my desire stokes the flame, burning me from the inside out.

Ren rips my new shirt right down the middle and quickly unzips the front of my sports bra, immediately homing in on my breasts. He tweaks one with his fingers, while his mouth engulfs the other, flicking it with his tongue and biting before switching to the other side.

Grabbing him by the back of his head, I twist my fingers into his hair so tightly, it must hurt. I'm practically shoving his face further into my boobs when he flips us back over and takes full control. Shoving his hard on directly into my core before licking down my body, following a trail of sweat from the exertion during our fight. His tongue trails over my belly button and down further. Yanking my spandex shorts down, he places his hulking form between my legs.

"Fucking beautiful." He reverently whispers to himself before fucking devouring me whole.

He doesn't hold back or tease me at all. He just licks, sucks and bites at my clit, then pushes two fingers into me, going right for my g-spot. I come so hard and so fast; I almost don't believe what just happened.

The aftershocks of my orgasm take over and my whole body disintegrates into goo.

And then, as if the flame is doused with water, common sense kicks in along with a crippling amount of guilt.

Cohen, Matteo, Noah.
Noah, Matteo, Cohen.

Over and over again, my brain chants their names and I push off of Ren, letting my guilt consume me.

"Oh my god, Ren. What did we just do? That's not even the first time you've touched me… and I've *let* you. What the fuck is wrong with me?" I ask, Nausea taking over my gut.

"I… I can't fucking do this." Running my fingers across my swollen lips and then pushing up off the ground, I snag up my shorts and put them back on as quickly as I can, not even taking an extra second to zip my bra back up, I take off in a dead sprint towards the upper levels of the house.

By the time I make it to my bedroom door, I notice that I'm definitely not alone. It's no doubt because his legs are double my length. I shift my body to his and push at his chest to let him know I don't want him in my space right now. He has that same presence that the guys did when they decided that we would all be together and I just can't fucking go through that again. Not right now. I can't give my heart away because they already fucking own it.

Hormones.

This is all just a stupid reaction to my god damn hormones. It isn't more than that.

It *can't* be more than that.

I don't understand why I keep caving to this staggering connection between the two of us, especially when I don't know where I stand with my guys. I left them with nothing. Not even a note. They either hate me or are going out of their minds looking for me, both of which are killing me inside. Guilt and resentment gnawing at my chest, weighing me down.

"Ren, please… Don't do this. Don't push for this. I. Love. *Them.* Nothing good can come from my being here. It's only going to hurt you. I don't want to hurt you; do you get that? Something inside of me connects to something inside of you, I won't deny that. But at the end of the day, I'm choosing them." I can only just get the words out, pushing them beyond the emotion clogging my throat.

"You. Are. Mine." He growls, and it's an echo of what Matteo once said to me, causing me to let out a weird noise as I barely restrain a sob that I will never let him see.

I knew love was weakness. I told them I didn't want this. I'm fucking stronger than this but fighting these feelings and missing them all at the same time is breaking me beyond anything I've ever experienced. I feel like a one woman shit show on display for everyone to see. I've never been this out of control.

Pulling myself together with the last ounce of inner strength I've got, I reach behind me and twist my doorknob, allowing the space to open up. I take a deep breath and look him dead in the eyes.

"I'm not yours. If you can't understand that I'm my own person and have to do things my own way, I'll never be yours." I say, and then push myself into my room and slam the door in his face before collapsing on the ground in front of my door and crying myself to sleep like I used to do when I was a little girl.

I wake up in the same spot I fell asleep. My eyes feel swollen and puffy, likely from my crying and a difficult sleep on the hardwood floor.

My body aches inside and out from the beating I've taken emotionally and physically. I almost don't pull myself up off the ground, but my stomach starts making gross noises, telling me how hungry I am. I have no idea what time it is, but I haven't eaten anything since my waffle breakfast before that emotionally charged work out. Was it earlier today or yesterday? Everything is foggy because of my emotional breakdown earlier.

Getting up off the floor, I walk over to my nightstand to check my alarm clock and see that it's just after eleven o'clock at night. I'm starving though, and my love of food is worth the risk of getting shot by a guard to sneak out of here for a midnight snack. Opening my door, I peek my head out to make sure that Ren is nowhere to be seen. I just can't deal with him right now. Once I've deemed the coast clear, I walk out of my room only to almost trip over a box. Curiosity wins and I pick it up, finding that it's fairly heavy, and go back into my room and sit on my bed.

I open the box and find most of my things in it. Not my gun or my knife, although that isn't surprising - I'm likely considered a flight risk, even though I'm almost sure we're on an island and I have no idea where. But my necklace and my phone, along with some snacks and drinks are in here.

This shows an incredible level of trust on Ren's part, if not a lot of stupidity. He knows how much I miss my life and my family. He knows now how deeply ingrained into my heart my guys are. He doesn't know about my necklace, but to give me my phone is a big step forward in gaining my trust and appreciation.

I care for him in ways I shouldn't and I can't even figure out why. It's like something in my heart just understands him on a whole other level. I know that it's wrong, but it's a gut feeling that I can't shake. I have my guys at the tips of my fingers now, just a phone call away, and yet, I'm torn when I didn't think I would be. Instinctively, I move to call the guys, but something stops me. Part of me wants to wait and see where my heart leads me with Ren. I don't owe him a chance to shoot his shot, but that's not exactly going to stop me from being led straight into his arms. So, placing my necklace back on my neck, I grasp it tightly and I call my mom instead.

TWELVE

ALESSANDRA

IT'S BEEN two whole weeks since I saw Ren last. I haven't even heard so much as a noise from his room or his office. He's given me full access to the house, but I can't bring myself to leave my room for anything other than food. I haven't even bothered working out, unable to deal with the memory of Ren's lips on me. I should be happy to have some distance, but something inside me feels utterly broken. It feels the same way I feel about being without Matteo, Noah and Cohen. Which is why I have yet to call them. I think maybe I just need this time to refocus on me instead of who I'm supposed to choose. Because if I *do* have to choose, I'll end up heart-broken either way.

My sleep is back to being troubled. Nightmares once again constantly battle my subconscious. During the day, my mind is stuck listening to the endless stream of thoughts that plague me, like a loop to the soundtrack of my life that just won't shut off. I'm still torn between the feelings that surface when he's near me and the guilt that torments me for having those feelings to begin with.

I've been through some seriously fucked up shit in my short life-time that hopefully most people never have to go through. I'm irrevocably damaged from a lifetime of pain - emotional and physical. It's what drives me; what causes me to be at the top of my game at all times. It's why, despite it being unconventional, my nonno felt he could make me his legacy. My life has made me who I am today and that person has never felt so alone or broken, despite the countless shit storms I've weathered.

I've never been a typical teenager, yet here I am, lost in a sea of emotions over four boys that somehow found their way into my heart. I thought I was crazy when I fell for *three* dudes and now I'm completely confused over a fourth. I finally called SB. After she cried and dramatically thanked every god known to mankind that I was okay all she said was,

"Damn girl, what are you even upset about? Four hot as fuck dudes want you. You legit have nothing to complain about. You're living every girls' fantasy right now... How many times have I asked you to switch lives with me? I mean, come on... Four. Hot. Guys... Four. Yes, please!"

And the crazy part is that she's not wrong. She never is, but apparently all I needed was to hear her voice chewing my ass out for overthinking this so hard. She also made several death threats toward the Gavino family, which cracked me up. Even though I know she wasn't entirely being serious, I still made sure to remind her how dangerous la famiglia is, how dangerous this whole situation actually is and to promise me not to say anything to anyone until I'm ready. Especially the boys.

My guys trust my judgement. I know that even the possessive assholes themselves wouldn't deny me the opportunity to fall in love with Ren if they thought it was something I really wanted to do. Their love is completely selfless. I'm the selfish one; keeping all of them to myself like I'm living a damn fantasy. We're still technically considered 'kids' for fuck's sake, despite not feeling like it or ever getting to act like it.

Maybe this is all for the best. Maybe I needed to be separated from them to gain some clarity and allow them the opportunity to move on if that's what they want. They deserve to be happy and find real, true love. Not some bullshit fantasy life that might never even really work. It seems damn near impossible to live that life without something falling apart, but I know now what I want and I have to hope for the best. I just hope that someday their hearts can learn to understand that this is how things are going to be now.

Although unexpected, I do have feelings for Ren and with that, I'll be losing some more of my independence, but gaining so much more. What the boys do with the news is up to them. I won't hold them back from moving on if they can't handle it. Now I just need to navigate this as best as I can.

With that, I make up my mind and open up my heart necklace and I push the button, nervous but sure. I trust my guys to have faith in my decision.

Knock, knock.

I hear James from the other side of my door. I don't want to talk to him so I burrow into my blankets, listening to him open up the door.

"Pardon, miss. The master would like to speak with you. Please make yourself presentable for dinner in an hour. You'll be served in the dining hall tonight." He says.

I grunt my acknowledgement, unsure if I can even form words at the moment. My heart is racing, whether in hope or fear of what I need to tell Ren, I have yet to determine.

Once I hear the door shut, I shoot up off the bed and run to the bathroom. Wallowing in self-pity from the confines of a room made for a queen, has allowed me to stay clean but I haven't exactly gone out of my way to take care of myself. Now that I've finally woken up and know exactly what I want. I need to make things right with Ren before the cavalry comes.

My mom and nonno are mostly aware of who I'm with and what I want, but when the guys inevitably come to them, they know the parts to play. At first they were furious when I told them everything, but they trust me enough to know that I'll call in our army if need be. And despite his love for me, I know nonno is thinking about how beneficial these ties can be for la famiglia. As a mob boss, it would be stupid of him not to.

For now, I'm just trying to figure out how to get what I want. I've never been able to have the freedom to just do what I want to do. It's always been what I needed to do to survive, but now things are different. Now I'm going to be someone's wife - multiple someone's at that if I get my way - and we won't take over the families yet, as the head of our families are all still alive, but we will make names for ourselves and we will own the entire damn underworld.

The path we've taken to get here may have gotten skewed along the way, but this was always inevitable. We have always been inevitable. Now that I'm starting to understand that on a deeper level, I'm so excited to see how things will change. The things we'll accomplish together will go down in history.

Walking down the stairs, I smell dinner before I make my way into the dining room, my stomach growls in hunger while simultaneously feeling like a swarm of butterflies has made a home there. I'm about to go in and make some heavy demands that may or may not backfire completely, but at least I'll know what to expect going forward.

As I enter the room I notice two things immediately. Someone is joining us for dinner and it's not a good thing. Ren isn't sitting at the head of the table as is expected, instead he's off to the right side of an older gentleman with silver hair and an ugly scowl. I can't see Ren's face but if the tautness of his shoulders and nefarious energy floating through the air are anything to go by, I'd say he's downright pissed off that this old guy is here.

"Ren... My love." I speak calmly and directly to Ren, as if to state that he's the only man who gathers my attention. If nothing else I know when to steel my spine and accept what the situation at hand is. Keeping my cards close to my chest won't hurt, but I will not cower to the man who has clearly taken charge of things here. This must be Raffaele Gavino. There's no doubt in my mind about that.

Ren looks to me and the relief and adoration that crosses his face is an immediate balm to my soul. He masks his face quickly, however, it's enough to calm me, even knowing this is likely going to end badly.

"Ren, won't you introduce me to your... associate?" I ask looking at him, purposefully demeaning Raffaele's position of authority by not giving the patriarch of the Gavino family my attention. He needs to understand that he's not the only person of power here. He may be the head of the mafia on the East coast, but my boss is Alessandro Salvatore and I don't show respect because it's expected. I show respect when it's earned.

I hold my hands out for him, showing a level of affection I have yet to in public. It clearly catches him off guard, as his eyes widen in surprise, but he quickly catches on that I'm willing to play the part for his sake. I know firsthand what's expected of us and how we are meant to be seen in front of *his* boss. Grandfather or not, la famiglia before family is more often than not the case in the life of the mob and I'm not willing to see him get hurt because I've decided to take things too far. I may not be willing to cower to this old man, but I will respect Ren for the kindness he's shown me since being here. Despite having been the wrong way to have gone about things, I'm here now and I'm considering marrying Ren, so let's see what the old man has to say.

"Mia bella, thank you for joining us for dinner. You look lovely. Please meet my grandfather, Raffaele Gavino." He says, while standing and moving to collect me from the doorway. His Italian accent coming through a bit stronger, giving away his nerves. He's calm on the outside, but his eyes show a simmering rage lies just beneath the surface of his easy going demeanor. He doesn't smile, and if not for his initial reaction to seeing me, I'd be confused as to who his anger is directed towards.

"I'm so sorry for this mi amore. He arrived unannounced. You're quite possibly about to see a side of me I'd wished to keep from you." He whispers, leaning down to place a gentle kiss on my lips before trying to step back away from me. Instead of letting him, I pull him in closer and deepen the kiss, opening my mouth and accepting his tongue against mine. If nothing else, I want this to be believable. His grandfather needs to believe that I'm falling in line. Plus, it's no hardship to kiss the fuck out of this super hot guy that I may or may not be genuinely interested in pursuing a relationship with.

Breaking away from the kiss, I'm breathless. I keep my forehead against his for a few more moments to catch my breath. The kiss itself was borderline inappropriate, but I needed Ren to understand that I'm here for him no matter what happens next.

"It's okay, let's get through this together and talk in *our* room tonight." I whisper back, looking him dead in the eye so that he fully understands how badly I need to speak with him privately before looking past him and finally greeting his grandpa.

"Hello sir, it's nice to finally meet you and put a face to the name." I smile just enough to be considered polite and offer a curt nod, but give nothing more, letting my face drop into a more passive look.

"Hm, let me get a good look at you, come, come." He snarls, watching each of my movements intently, not bothering to conceal his judgements.

I look to Ren and then back to the old man. Forcing my legs to move toward him, refusing to show even an ounce of fear or hesitation.

This man is used to people fearing him. I'm not one willing to be afraid of many things outside of my own heart. Ren tightens his grip on my hands as though he doesn't want me to go. He knows something is wrong too. I pull him along with me, keeping him close and doing my best to ease his mind as we get closer to the menacing old man before us. When we come to a stop Raffaele leers at me, slowly taking me in from head to toe, and apparently finds me lacking.

"Mi aspettavo di più da un Salvatore. Non è abbastanza brava." He says, his scowl taking over his entire face.

I'm not fluent, but I'm not stupid either and I've picked up quite a bit of Italian from what my own nonno has taught me. I'm fairly certain he said he expected more from a Salvatore and that I'm not good enough for his grandson. Fucking dickhead.

"Abbastanza nonno! Deve essere mia moglie. Nemmeno tu mancherai di rispetto ai contatti tra famiglie. Lei è in debito con me. Ho intenzione di tenerla!" Ren shouts.

I'm not prepared for him to start yelling, but when he does, I find myself surprised. Not many people are willing to speak to a mob boss like that and I imagine if anyone else were here, there's no question that it wouldn't be happening. He's getting a pass for being family, but from the look and his grandpa's face he's about to find himself six feet under so I turn and face him, reaching my hand up to place it over his fast beating heart.

"Shh... Va tutto bene. Sono tuo - it's okay, I'm yours. Ren, I'm yours. Calm down." I say firm, but quiet. They have to stop yelling at each other to hear me, which is exactly what I was hoping for as I turn my glare to Raffaele.

"I may not be everything you expected for your grandson, but I'm what you've got. I'm what he wants and I'm what's already been bartered for. I've finally accepted what's to come so leave us be and we'll make the arrangements on our own." I say, staring him down, letting him know he doesn't intimidate me. He sure as shit doesn't deserve my respect, so he damn well won't be getting it. I continue to stare into Ren's gaze, wanting him to fully understand my meaning.

"Hmm, so you're prepared to marry my grandson then? You're prepared to give up your own legacy and become a wife? You will have a role to play and it's not one you've envisioned; of that I can guarantee." He laughs at me, like this is all some game and not our fucking lives. It's enough to get me to turn my glare on him.

"We have time to decide what we want to do and how we are to go about it. That's not up to you. Neither of us are even eighteen yet so it's not like we can get married tomorrow. Let us take the time we need to get to know each other and... I don't know, date? Also, no offense, but you're in-fucking-sane if you think I'm going to sit back and be someone's little housewife. I'm to be an Underboss in my own right, under my grandfather, Alessandro Salvatore, when I turn eighteen. I'll agree to marrying Ren, there's no doubt in my mind that it's the right thing to do, but I have my own conditions." I seethe.

"For someone who's gotten as far in life as you have, you'd think you'd understand how these things work a lot better. First of all, you have as much time as I'm willing to give you. No more. No less. You don't get to have conditions. You are not in charge here. Your grandfather and I will speak and come to an agreement on how you will best proceed as a wife, not an Underboss, that's laughable. You are a woman. You are meant to bed your husband and breed the future generation. You are to be seen, not heard. You tend to the house and you feed your family. That is how things are done. Contractually, you belong to my grandson and you will do as you are told or you will die. It is all very simple you see." He looks as though he's attempting to smile, though it comes out as more of a grimace.

It's ugly and nauseating. For now though, I prefer him to think he has the upper hand. I knew that everything he said was what's expected. I won't comply as he'd like, but he doesn't need to know that yet. And nonno won't agree to any of that. He's old fashioned in business, but ruthlessly protective in family matters.

"I see. Well, then I shall leave you both to your dinner. If you'll excuse me. Ren, I'll see you in our bedroom. Hurry this along if you can." I give him a light peck on his lips and turn to leave them to tend to their business. With any luck, Ren will have his grandfather gone by the end of tonight.

"Ah, ah, ah! Just a moment dear. You'll have to bear with us a short while longer. There's much left to be done tonight. Don't you know that it's my grandson's birthday? It's a celebrazione!" Raffaele's vile grimace widens into a full smile, and it's evil in every sense of the word.

When another person enters the room and I look to see someone I would've never expected. Looking up to Ren, I do my best to hide my panic. When he tries to mouth to me how sorry he is, I know I have to make some big decisions here.

I fucking *knew* it! I knew deep in my bones that nothing good would come from Raffaele Gavino showing up.

"So there is... I guess we better get to it then. Happy birthday il mio re." I look to Ren first, to show him that I'm ok and then to Raffaele, smiling like he isn't fucking up all of my plans. This piece of shit won't get to see me sweat, even as his sickening voice wafts over me.

"And so we shall..."

THIRTEEN

ALESSANDRA

I MAKE my way around Ren's room. Not exactly snooping, as tempting as that might be. Just getting a feel for things. For some reason, I expected his space to be dark and brooding, everything black, or red even. Maybe leather furniture or even more of the dungeon-y feel I got from my first experience here. It's all decorated in various shades of blue, however. Intricate artwork decorates the walls, and pictures of me are framed on his bedside table. Not like a shrine, as I imagined before I knew him. Just a simple set of photos taken of me laughing or smiling.

The decor is color coordinated in a way that it almost entirely matches the spectacular view from his floor to ceiling window, which faces the ocean and sandy beaches that span for miles. Wherever it is that we are, I can't deny its beauty.

I step into the walk-in closet and find that he wasn't joking when he said I have an entire wardrobe here. Grabbing a pair of modest panties and one of his t-shirts instead, I move out of the expansive space and back over to the bed to lay out the clothes I've chosen for bed.

I'm facing away from the door and just get the shoulder of

my dress pushed down when I hear the door creak open. I stiffen slightly, as I look over my shoulder to see Ren standing in the doorway staring at me with lust-fueled eyes.

"I'll come back. Go ahead and change." He says, unmoving, allowing himself a moment to drink me in.

"It's okay, Ren. I trust you. Come in. I could probably use some help with my zipper anyway. One of the maids was kind enough to help me into this dress, but there's no way I'm getting out of it on my own." I say, genuinely meaning it. I do trust him. He messed up, going about things the way that he did, but I understand it so much more now. The pull that he felt. The draw to me, like I feel for him and the guys.

"I really shouldn't, Quinn. I don't know if I have much self-control left to offer you. I haven't seen you in two weeks and now with the circumstances what they are... Not to mention that I've damn near driven myself mad with need for you. To see you. To touch you. Fuck... To *taste* you."

And even though the words he's saying tell me that he needs to stay away, he still moves closer. It's only a moment before I feel him at my back and his hands firmly grasp my hips.

Tilting my head back, I meet his lips with my own, then turn to face him to continue the passionate dance our tongues are creating. Reaching my hands up to grasp his face, I pull him in closer. The need to be pressed against him is immediate and insistent. He reciprocates by grabbing my ass and lifting my legs up around his waist, then shifting us onto the bed with the brunt of his weight coming down on me.

Tilting my hips up, I grind myself against his erection, practically begging for his dick with the motions of my body. I allow myself a few more moments of pure bliss in his arms before trying to pull away. He follows me and continues to kiss me so deeply; I can practically feel him telling me how much he cares about me with that kiss alone.

"Wait, Ren. Slow down. A lot's been said tonight and I need to make sure you understand the conditions in which I agreed to all of this. Your grandfather may not accept them, but he's the least of my concerns. Do you understand what I need from you?" I push at his chest lightly. Not so he leaves my personal space, but just enough that I can look him in the eyes and convey how deadly serious I am.

"I need *you* to understand something, mi amore. I'm willing to try to give you what you want. It won't be easy, but I've realized that I'd rather give you what you need than lose you altogether. I can't guarantee that it will go smoothly. I'm a jealous fucker and I've never wanted *anything* the way I want you. You are it for me. I just wish I were enough for you too."

"Ren, stop. That's not fair... If I had to live the rest of my life with you and only you, I could, but I wouldn't feel complete, if that makes sense. I never had any control over falling in love with them, just like you had no control over falling in love with me. It just happened. And while *our* connection is strong, so is my connection to them. It means more than I could ever say that you've agreed to try. Especially now." I press a kiss to his lips and pull back, wincing slightly at the look of concern he shows at my words.

"What does that mean? Especially now. Quinn..." His voice trails off and I know he knows I'm about to throw down something majorly conflicting.

"Ren, I need to tell you something. I've done something that you may have expected. Maybe you actually trusted me *not* to do it, I don't really know to be honest."

"You called them didn't you? You're about to tell me that you want to go back to them. Even after everything that's just happened? You came up here and immediately called to grovel and beg their forgiveness, huh?" He pushes off of me and rolls over to look at the ceiling and then petulantly throws his arm over his eyes, pouting like he's already lost his chance with me.

I'm not willing to let him go that easily though. Not now that I've accepted this to be our reality.

"No. Ren, I didn't come straight up here to call them. I haven't spoken with them since the night before I left home to cross the country on my own to figure out who you were." I roll my body into his side, peering up to look at his handsome face, even though half of it is covered with his forearm. He moves his arm just enough to look down at me with one uncovered eye, looking for signs of a lie.

"So, what then? What did you do? And I know that you've done something, so don't try to tell me you haven't. You might be able to fool everyone else, but not me. I know you probably better than you even know yourself." He's serious, and the vulnerability in his voice tells me that even though neither of us were truly given a choice in the matter, right now he needs me to lay everything out on the table for him. He needs me to choose him in this moment. Maybe nobody ever really has. His life until this point hasn't been about love, true loyalty and family. It's been an obligation on gaining honor among criminals.

"Ren, look at me." I say as I pull myself up onto my elbow and move his arm from his face to look him in the eye.

"Hey, I won't ever lie to you. Yes, I've chosen you for a lifetime... But I'm choosing them too. I didn't call them on the phone, no. I called out to their location detectors. I sent them my exact location via GPS. They are probably already on their way here."

"You did what?! How? I disabled your phone's location settings myself. There's no way you could've done that. Why would you do this? After tonight especially. You should have talked to me first. This is something that we should be working through together. This is something that we should be talking to them about together. I haven't even gotten time with you yet. Fuck! I wanted to get real one on one time with you before we brought them back into the fold. They got you for months! I've only just come to terms with sharing you and now I don't even fucking get a moment to enjoy this with you. Questa è una tale cazzata!!" He jumps up off the bed and starts pacing and mumbling in Italian so fast, I can't even pretend to know what he's saying. I just know that he's mad and it's hot as fuck. He pulls his gun from his waistband and I realize why I'm falling for him. He looks like a psychopath right now. His crazy matches my crazy. I'm now positive that I'm fucked in the head.

He holds his gun and aims at the bathroom door before letting off three shots into it.

"Ren! What the fuck are you doing?" I run to him and lower the gun to aim it at the floor before disarming him completely. He doesn't even put up a fight as I take the gun, instead letting it go and moving to the wall and throwing punches into it. I stand back and let him wreak his havoc. He needs to be angry right now. He just won't be doing it with a gun.

"Ren? Hey, il mio re. Look at me. Everything is going to be okay. I don't want them to know everything just yet. Can you keep tonight a secret for now? At least until I figure out how to explain it all to them. We'll tell them that we're together for now, but the rest needs to wait until we can all figure out how to make this work beyond your grandfather's misogynistic, archaic ways of viewing our world. I know they'll understand. They'll be pissed at first, because they've been lied to their whole lives, too. And well, you know, the kidnapping. Also, maybe that I've essentially built myself a harem of men and then added another guy without talking to them first like a total asshole... God, I'm a selfish dick, huh?" I look to him and smile, hopefully getting through to him.

"I could never fully commit to you knowing that I just gave up on them. That's not love. Love is hard. Emotionally, they'd always have a piece of me and you'd grow to resent me for it. I didn't know it until I was with you that there was a piece missing to complete me, but I do now. It's how I know that I'm supposed to be with you, but without them, it's not whole, either. I just can't be complete without *all* of you." I move back to him, grabbing for his injured hands. I bring the busted knuckles up to my mouth and place soothing, gentle kisses on each one of them.

"Let me grab a first aid kit so we can get this cleaned up. I know you're upset with me, but we can make this work if you're still willing to try."

I go to the bathroom and look in the cabinet for a first aid kit, and hear Ren follow me in and turn on the shower. When I turn around to look at him, he's got his shirt off and he's unzipping his pants. I've been thankful for his self-restraint, but I can now see the toll it's taking on him. He's hard as a rock in his tight black boxer briefs and I start to worry I might start drooling if I don't stop staring.

"Uhh, do you, um..." Shit, I gotta get it together, but god *damn*. How on earth did I get lucky enough to attract the attention of a man that looks like a tattooed Adonis? Blinking rapidly to shake off my look of desperation, I look at his face.

"Would you like me to clean your cuts before you shower? Or if you'd prefer, I can go wait for you and bandage them when you're done."

Instead of answering me, he stalks to me as if he's a predator on the prowl. He's angry and turned on. He's hot and hard all over and the closer he gets to me, the more my body starts to shiver in response. Most women would be scared from the look on his face, except I'm not normal and all this is doing is turning me the fuck on. Apparently my body still has *some* natural protective instinct though because next thing I know, I'm backed up against the bathroom door without remembering taking the steps to get here. Ren uses his knee to widen my stance and he steps in between my legs, pushing his erect dick directly into my hot center while grasping my legs to wrap around him. If not for his underwear, I swear he'd be balls deep in me right now, and I'm not even sure if I'd be upset about it. Every ounce of energy that seeps from him is a threat, a warning. He's dangerous right now and I'm sick in the head for wanting every bit of his menace as he drags his rough, bloody knuckles down my face.

"So, I'm supposed to do what then? Share you? You want us all to take turns or do you want us all at the same time?" He growls and my body involuntarily shakes with need.

"Does it turn you on thinking about all of us sinking our cocks into each of your holes? Are you wet right now?" He asks, as he reaches down between us and pushes my panties aside while I swallow the moan that wants to escape. He swirls two fingers around my clit before dipping them into my dripping cunt. He can feel how wet and swollen I am, turned on by his words and calloused touches; my need for release is as clear as day and a spark of mischief lights up his dark eyes.

"And what if I've changed my mind and say no? What happens then? What if I force you to stay locked up, keeping you all to myself? You're all mine right now. I could just take us away from here and hide you away a while longer. Or I could just take you here and now. Claim what's rightfully *mine*." His dark rasp causes goosebumps to roll over my body. Whimpers of pleasure tumble from my mouth as he pumps his fingers in and out of me, curling up into the perfect spot and bringing me to the brink of orgasm despite the frustration I feel at his words.

"What happens then, hmm? What is it about me that's not enough for you? Are you worried I can't pleasure you like they do?" He growls before kissing the fuck out of me, biting my lips just enough to draw blood and add a little pain to my pleasure.

"Fucking watch me."

"Ohhh... Fuck! Ren!" An orgasm seizes me in that moment and it's so powerful, I can hardly believe he did it with just his fingers. My pussy tightly squeezes his fingers as the aftershocks ripple through me. It takes a few extra minutes for my breathing to return to normal and my pussy to stop convulsing. When it does, he pulls his fingers out of me and brings them to my lips, rubbing my juices across my swollen lips, then leaning in to trace his tongue along my mouth, licking up my essence.

Violence pours off of him in waves, he's practically frantic with an unmatched savage energy. I reach my hands up to cup his face, looking up at him, genuinely concerned with what he said.

"Is that really what you're worried about? That you aren't enough? Ren, clearly you can fulfill my physical needs. I'm obviously attracted to you. Listen to me. You're one hundred percent enough to make me feel good. It's not about competing with one another for my attention. It's about the connection I have with each of you. I've spent my entire life fighting off men and hiding from the attention they give me. I couldn't do that with any of you. It's like each of you are a part of me. We are connected. Without all of you, I'm not whole." He drops his forehead to mine, his chest heaving with each breath he takes as he tries to calm himself.

"I get that, or at least I'm starting to. You need to understand how hard this all is for me though as well. I honestly have no idea how to do that when I've spent my entire life thinking that you were mine. *Only* mine. Just the thought of someone else touching you makes me fucking crazy. I don't think you fully understand the level of psychosis I can reach. I get murderous."

"Don't make me choose. Trust me when I tell you that you won't like the answer. If you ask me to give them up, I'll never be able to forgive you. I know what I'm asking for is selfish. I can't help that it's how I feel though. Just- look, let's focus on us until they get here an-" I'm cut off by him slamming his lips into mine with another brutal kiss. It's harsh and full of dominating promise.

"No... I'm claiming you here. Now. You're fucking *mine*."

It's that moment that I realize he's dropped his underwear because he rubs the head of his dick against my still wet pussy. Oh, fuck. He's gonna-

"Ugh!" I make an ugly sound as he jerks one of my legs back up around his waist and slams into me without any other warning. Fuck that hurts! It happens so fast; I feel my eyes involuntarily start to water and I can hardly catch my breath before he crushes his lips back onto mine. He doesn't even wait to allow me to adjust to his intrusion as he starts to move in and out of me with abandon, setting a punishing rhythm that causes pleasure to start chasing away the pain and eliciting a whimper from me that gives away my feeling of uncertainty from what's happening right now.

He pulls his mouth from mine and looks at me with wild obsession coloring his gaze. His whole face lights up with concern at what he must see though because he jerks himself out of me and swoops me up like he's a husband carrying his new bride across their threshold and carries me back to the bedroom where he gently lays me down on the bed. The change in his demeanor seriously throws me off when I see the amount of love that reflects back at me, sending tingles down my spine and further confusing my complicated feelings.

"Mi dispiace tanto amore mio. I'm so, so fucking sorry. I was too rough with you. I should've never let my temper get the best of me. You deserve so much more for our first time. I'll do better, mi amore. Ti amo." He whispers the words into my ear and brushes hair from my face, looking at me like I hung the moon and stars.

Laying himself over me on the bed, he slowly pushes himself back into me, creating a glorious friction between the two of us as his pace quickens. Every time he pushes back inside, he swivels his hips so that he grinds himself so perfectly against me that I think I might die from the overwhelming pleasure it causes. I'm practically breathless when I finally give him a response.

"I'm ok, just keep going. It feels so fucking good. Don't stop. *Please.*" I'm finally beyond the pain, all-consuming need taking its place as I beg for him to keep moving. I find myself pushing myself onto him, meeting him thrust for thrust, clenching around his length. It causes him to let out a long groan that turns me on even more.

I grab him by the back of his neck and pull him back into a kiss, taking control of it. I swirl my tongue around his at the same rhythm that I'm grinding myself on him.

"That's it baby, fucking use me. Get off on my dick." He moans into my mouth, letting some of the Italian flow free as he loses himself to the passion between us. His words have me squeezing myself even tighter around him. God, the dirty talk mixed with his beautiful Italian language is practically my undoing.

"Come on mi amore, come with me." He moves faster, hitting a spot in me I didn't know existed at the same time that he reaches down and rubs my clit, causing me to practically weep from the staggering amount of pleasure that washes over me. I feel him swell inside of me as he pushes inside deep for the last time, holding his body against mine like he never wants to leave. I smile up at him deliriously as my body comes down from the high it's on.

When he finally pulls out of me, I wince slightly at the pain and from the mess I can feel leaking out of me. I know I shouldn't be embarrassed, but I know that there's a flush across my cheeks that I can't hide when he rubs his cum into my skin, pushing it back into me, claiming me with his seed.

I watch him curiously as he becomes mesmerized while playing with my body, turning us both back on in the process. I find it hard to believe that he's this consumed with my body, but then he speaks and I stare in disbelief as he pumps his hand along his hardened length again.

"We're definitely gonna have to do that again."

FOURTEEN

ALESSANDRA

"WHAT. THE. ACTUAL. *FUCK*!"

I wake up to a chorus of thunderous, raging voices, and my whole body stiffens when I recognize who they belong to. I know how this situation looks, too. I'm all wrapped up in Ren, fully naked and one hundred percent sure I have sex hair like nobody's business. I didn't realize it would take them so little time to get here. I guess that was dumb of me, considering I still don't know where *here* is. Of course they figured out how to bypass the guards to get in here. These guys are smarter and more diligent than a well-trained army. I just hope they haven't left anyone dead.

I fucked up real big this time. I let my need to reassure Ren take over and in doing so, I know I'm at risk of losing them all. Maybe I should've called and talked to them first, because if the roles were reversed I'd be feeling murderous and heartbroken.

"Everyone calm down!" I yell, sitting up quickly, accidentally letting the sheet slip down my body, exposing my bare breasts. My nipples harden in response to the chill of the air as well as having four pairs of eyes zero in on my breasts.

Reaching down, I grab for the sheets to cover myself up if for no other reason than to take back a little control. Taking a deep breath and steeling my spine looking around to see Ren with his gun raised and pointed at Cohen, and Noah with his gun raised at Ren. Where in the fuck did Ren even pull a gun from? Matteo is looking simultaneously furious and shocked now that he's taken notice of his twin.

"Put the fucking guns down. Right. The fuck. Now." I glare at all of them.

"Look, we have a lot to talk about. I know how this looks. I know this is bad. Just- Will you let me explain some shit?" I look at each of them, noting how Cohen has dark circles under his eyes, he hasn't been sleeping. Noah's hair is growing out like crazy and he looks sort of twitchy, like he's struggling to contain his demons. Matteo's beard has definitely grown out, but he's also looking far from his normal calm, careful stoicism. Each of them actually looks defeated, if not slightly angsty and trigger happy.

I move to stand, and get yanked back onto the bed by Ren, causing every other man in the room to growl and step forward protectively.

"Let go Ren. Seriously. We've already talked about the possessive macho man bullshit. You knew what was coming. Put your ego aside and let me get dressed so we can all try to have a civilized conversation. Think about how blindsided these guys must be to see you and our compromising position when they have no idea what's going on, and likely thought they were coming to save me. How would you feel if the roles were reversed?" I whisper for only his ears, and surprisingly, he listens. Only releasing a small growl to further show his frustration.

I stand up and refuse to allow my nakedness to be awkward. If this works out the way I hope it will, they'll all have to get used to me being naked in front of each other anyway.

Making my way into the walk-in closet, I send a silent prayer to Buddha that they don't kill each other while I'm dressing. I grab some joggers and one of Ren's t-shirts, throwing everything on haphazardly and then make my way back out, grabbing some basketball shorts for Ren at the last moment and throwing them to him from the doorway.

I get swept up in an unexpected hug by Noah, and I bury my face in his neck to breathe in his delicious scent, while also buying myself a moment so I don't cry like a little bitch right now.

"I've been so worried, Feisty. Don't you ever fucking leave me like that again. Don't you know that I'll always follow you? I love you beyond obsession and I'll never let you leave me again. I would burn the world to the ground looking for you." His voice sounds so morose that I feel every ounce of his pain like it's my own.

"I can't wait to spank your ass for all this shit you put us through. We all know how good red looks on you." He says darkly, just before I feel Cohen's arms wrap around me from behind. This right here, between them, this is definitely my happy place, and it calms some of the storm raging in my heart. Their existence is a balm to my soul.

"If this is all what I think it is, just keep in mind that this will affect Matteo the hardest. Finding you like this changes nothing for me, Q. I love you more today, than I did the day you disappeared. You're it for me. But hear me when I tell you this, you will never leave us like that again. I have very little issue leaving a trail of bodies in our wake to hunt you down. We would've gone to the ends of the earth to find you. At some point you have to stop underestimating our love for you." He says into the spot he knows I love on my neck, just under my ear. His voice and soft breath sending shivers down my spine.

"Smart move, making our watches GPS trackers for your necklace. The engraving makes even more sense now." He places a gentle kiss on my neck and then nips at my ear before releasing his arms from around my stomach, while Noah turns me around, allowing me to walk to 'Teo.

My movements are slow and methodical. I keep my eyes trained on his face, even though his gaze is bouncing back and forth between his brother and myself. He's trying to make sense of it and I can see his mind moving a million miles a minute trying to process the unbelievable sight before him. When I finally reach him, I have his full attention, but he's guarded. Not open and possessive like he usually is with me. If looks could kill, though...

"Hi 'Teo." I try and talk above a whisper, but my voice has other plans. Showing a vulnerability I don't often, I look to him openly and let my honesty shine through.

"I know this looks so bad, like legit, fucked up. I completely understand how mad you must be, but are you willing to listen to our story to understand everything that's happening?"

I don't even think I deserve this chance with them to be honest. How could I betray them so easily and then hope for forgiveness. I am the epitome of scum. I'm the fucking worst, and I know it.

"Are you really going to stand there and try to justify whatever the fuck I just walked in on? I gave- *we* gave you every piece of ourselves. We let you into our world, into our hearts and we fucking trusted you, only to find you naked as fuck, in bed with some wannabe bad boy." He growls.

"Here we are, thinking we needed to save you from my dad, only to find you naked with some guy with *my* goddamn face! What am I even supposed to do with that?!" He's fuming, and understandably so.

"How could you fuck him? You're *mine*! Ours. Or at least, I thought you were. I guess I had that all the way wrong. I guess it's true what they say, loving someone gives them the biggest opportunity to hurt you. It was stupid of me to think you never would. I should've known that loving you would hurt like hell..." His voice trails off, allowing me to tap into the hurt that I caused. Then before I can get a word in, he starts to walk away.

I can't let that happen. I won't let him go without a fight, even as selfish as I know that is. I move quickly and grab his arm, only for him to flip me around and smash me into the door so hard, it rattles and shakes as my head bounces off of it. I don't need to see it to know that I'm bleeding now. Adrenaline surges through me and I punch him directly in the face, landing a decent right hook on his jaw. Bringing my left fist up to guard my face, I move to hit him again, but he slaps my hand away and puts his face right up in mine. I can hear Ren start to lose his cool in the background and know that Noah and Cohen must have stepped in and are holding him back from coming to my rescue.

What Ren doesn't know is that as pissed as Matteo is, he'd never purposefully hurt me, he just can't see beyond the pain and the anger. What none of them might realize is that I need this as much as 'Teo does.

I glare up at him and feel his hatred seep into me like poison. He looks like a raging bull, with his nostrils flaring and his eyes narrowed into a fierce glare. His breathing is becoming more labored as everything starts to weigh on him, without him being able to fully connect the pieces. I can see it all laid out as the gears spin in his mind.

"Fuck you, Alessandra. If I'm so easily replaceable then let me go and live your happily ever after in your castle on the sea. I thought I knew you, but clearly I fucking don't. You're just another bitch who'll take a ride on the first dick that gives you an ounce of attention. You really are just trash, nothing but a fucking whore."

Wow, I know I deserve that, but fuck him for thinking he can say that shit to me. I hit him again. This time I clip his mouth and when it starts to bleed, I smirk, but not in a good way. No, my smile is ugly and mean as hell. This is the fight that I need from him and I want it to hurt.

"Huh, I didn't take you for such a little bitch, your majesty. Who knew you'd just give up on what we have just because you feel scared, no, not scared, *threatened*. That's it right? You're afraid of what you don't know, and that guy with your face, he's what's got you all in your own head. Not because I fucked him, but because it's fucking with you to be in the dark about something. You can talk all the shit you want about how you don't know me, but you do, and you know I'd never do anything that I didn't think you'd agree to. I fucking love you, you stupid asshole. Yeah, so he 'got' my virginity, who cares? It's just some archaic idea of ownership that's total bullshit. Boo-fucking-hoo. It was never anyone's to take. It was always mine to give.

"You get *me*. All of me. For-fucking-ever. And that should be enough for you. It would've been once. So what fucking changed? Thinking you've been replaced? I'd never replace you, you stupid, stubborn ass. But you'd rather run away than listen to a goddamn explanation or let yourself open up for me again. So, go on then, *leave*. Take the easy way out. I won't stop you again. If you know anything about me, it's that I will *always* out stubborn you. This is the last chance you'll get from me."

"Aaaggghhh!" He screams and then shoves his fist into the door, less than an inch from my face. I don't expect it, but I don't flinch either. If he walks away, he doesn't get to see me fall apart. I won't put that on him and guilt him into staying. I also won't show him the fear he clearly wants from me right now. He doesn't scare me though. I trust him with everything that I am. Ren doesn't though, and before I can register what's happened, he's yanked him backwards and swept 'Teo's legs out from under him, pummeling his face before 'Teo even fully hits the ground.

"Don't you fucking touch her!" He growls between harsh panting breaths. His wrath flowing free, creating a toxic energy that buzzes throughout the room.

Matteo gets in a few hits before he throws his weight into Ren and bucks him off. They both bounce up onto their feet and square up like this will be the fight of the century and as hot as it is to see them ready to fight, I don't want it to be against each other. I know they'll kill one another if I don't put a stop to it.

They begin to circle each other, looking with matching calculated eyes for a weak spot to strike the other. Ren throws a punch at the same time Matteo kicks at Ren's kidneys. Neither of them land their strikes. Both shift back to reevaluate how to move in again, leaving an opening for me to step in between the two of them.

"Stop!" I yell, holding my hands up to both of them.

"You guys need to fucking chill." This situation is already so much more unreal than I ever expected, blood and violence making itself well known here.

"Ren, this is not the way to officially meet him and all of that was uncalled for. He would never actually hurt me. Can't you see that he's the one hurting?" I tell him, then shift my focus from one brother to the next.

"'Teo, calm the fuck down. Ren has played his part in this, but he wasn't the instigator. All of this shit started with your dad, Lorenzo Deluca, *Senior*. Matteo, Ren is short for Lorenzo, as in Lorenzo DeLuca Jr. Ren is your brother, only older than you by a few minutes and he has been raised by your mother's family- your real mother's family, the Gavino's. You've heard of them, I know you have, because I have. The contract your father brought to your attention back home, you know, the one that made you think you could lay claim on me in the first place? The one that promises me to the DeLuca heir, well, it actually says I am contractually bound to the *eldest* DeLuca son. Which everyone overlooked because anyone that knows the DeLuca family on the entire West coast is under the impression that there is only one DeLuca heir."

FIFTEEN

ALESSANDRA

"NO. No fucking way. That's such bullshit. My dad is a dickhead. He's the epitome of a dirtbag; king of the douchebags. I get that, but my mom… I mean, she was my fucking mom. She was all I fucking had growing up. I- Just no…" He looks at me, clearly heartbroken at the idea that his mom wasn't truly his mom. It's as though he wishes I could change it all for him. Like, maybe rewind the clock and take us back to when we were ignorant and happy. I've never seen him look so emotionally damaged. This is my indestructible man. Never one to let his damage show, he's been hard as stone since I met him. Full of pride unlike anything I've ever known. It's conflicting as hell to see him look so broken when I know there's absolutely no way to fix it.

"Quinn isn't lying to you, asshole. Why would she? I can have my mom here by the afternoon with all of the hospital documentation if you really need proof. As if my face isn't enough." He scoffs.

"Though, I'm sure she'd love to meet you. All she's been able to do all these years is get updates through Lorenzo, and I'm sure you can guess how forthcoming he's been. Honestly, he's everything you said and more. If I ever see him again, I'll kill him with my bare fucking hands." Ren is clearly forcing the words out at this point. His hatred for his father, his having to learn how to share me and with his twin brother of all people, it might be too much for him seeing as it's clearly getting to him.

Matteo just being here seems to be a problem for him. He obviously doesn't like him, but is it all because of me or is there more to it? He almost sounds jealous at the idea of letting Matteo meet his real mom. I can't imagine how it must feel to have someone swoop in and have the ability to lay claim to the only things in the world that you love, especially knowing that they already love the person threatening to claim them.

"That's actually not the worst idea. Not only could it help us figure out a lot of the missing pieces to this puzzle, it could really help all three of you start to gain some understanding of each other and maybe start to heal you all a little bit. Plus, I'm sure your mom has missed 'Teo all of these years. I can't imagine it would be easy to give your son up to another woman and such a disgusting excuse of a man." Cohen says, forever the levelheaded one. I notice he's also keeping a calculated eye on the twins. More so on Ren. My sweet Cohen can't help himself. He's as inquisitive as me, if not more. If he doesn't understand something, he studies it, dissects it, learns it and controls it.

"No. Fuck that. I had a mom. I had an amazing fucking mom who loved me and did everything she could to protect me from that monster. That woman raised me and she never would've lied to me like that. This can't be real. Even if it is, I won't replace her with some dumb bitch that would willingly give me up to a guy as evil as Lorenzo fucking DeLuca." Teo seethes.

"Watch your fucking mouth about my mother. I won't tell you again. You may be my blood, but you aren't my brother. I've put people in the ground for showing less disrespect to mia momma." Ren snarls.

"Non mi dispiacerebbe ucciderti adesso come è" The intimidating low rumble of Italian flows from his mouth as though he doesn't have a care in the world that these boys likely know what he said and that he'll definitely piss off three guys just as big as him. I may not know much, but the boys seem to have understood him and if I'm right, I think he definitely made a death threat. Three against one odds aren't good, yet he seems completely confident with his choice of words.

I should've known this would happen. Hell, I *did* know this would happen, and I'm a sick bitch for loving being in the center of all of this animosity. I have goosebumps all over from the thick brooding masculinity in the air.

"Watch your fucking mouth. You aren't the only one with blood on your hands. He may not be *your* brother, but he *is* mine, and I too have put people in the ground for less." Noah states softly, remaining eerily calm. The only hint that he is going to his dark place is his quiet demeanor. My normally sarcastic, happy-go-lucky guy is nowhere to be seen. In his place the viciousness that I know he hides well is coming out to play. My Jekyll and Hyde. He's my favorite brand of crazy.

While I typically love the testosterone fueled madness that overcomes my guys as they get worked up for a fight, I'd prefer it if they weren't making enemies of each other. It's time to deescalate the situation a bit because the amount of hatred bleeding from their pores, while they stare each other down is palpable. Ren and Matteo look like they're about to internally combust. Noah is clearly losing his grip on the short fuse he has at the best of times, and Cohen is simply assessing the situation, but I have no doubt that he'd jump into the fight to protect his brother if necessary. He likely already has seen at least five different outcomes in his head as it is. The adrenaline thrumming through my body from all this fighting is starting to cloud my own judgement, so I can't imagine it's doing anything good for the boys. We need to clear the air, and with these boys, I know just the way to do it.

Watching these guys beat the ever living fuck out of each other is like my every fantasy come to life. I'm watching the sweat pour off of them as they go pound for pound on the mats. I was adamant that they wear gear and follow boxing regulations.

Normally I wouldn't care if they wanted to fight dirty, but there's no trust here, and until there is, it's gonna be nothing but clean fights. No hitting below the belt, no kidney shots and they are only allowed to strike with a closed fist. No MMA shit. No groundwork at all, and under no circumstance are they allowed to strike while their opponent is down. Those are the rules. Those are *my* rules. If they break the rules, they fight *me*. They need this, though. These guys are all more similar than they realize. It took me a long time to understand how much they're like me too. The fight will help. It always helps me.

After watching them for some time, I'm itching to hit the mats. Except I'm worried that if I walk away to change, everything will go to shit. I don't think I can trust these guys alone just yet. I'm not a shrink though, so what the hell do I know?

Ehh, fuck it. They're all big boys. They can handle themselves without me babysitting them. If they can't respect my rules, I'll happily kick the shit out of all of them. I look back one last time, smirking at how hard they are trying to hold back just to prove that they can. The sparring hasn't been bad so far, but only because I paired Ren up with Cohen, and if anyone here has the capability of staying levelheaded enough to fight him, it's Cohen. The hostility is growing between the twins though and I can feel it all coming to a head, likely sooner rather than later.

When I reach the lockers I look around and find a pair of skintight spandex shorts and a sports bra. I don't want to hit the mats with any loose clothing on my body that they can grab at and use for leverage. Sparring with them is fun, but I know my guys and they fight dirty, especially with me. I don't have a brush or anything so I finger comb my unruly mess of hair into a high pony and let it hang down my back. I forego socks and shoes, even though some of these kicks are begging for me to show them some love. I'm pretty sure I saw a pair of Nike Zoom Kobe Six's over there. Yeah, those limited edition beauties are calling my name. But not right now. I gotta tape up and get back to my guys.

By the time I'm all taped up and walking back to them, I notice that the partners have been switched up. Nope, scratch that. Cohen and Noah are standing off to the side at this point watching Matteo and Ren pound each other into oblivion. Matteo already has a black eye that's starting to swell and Ren's lip is busted. These guys are basically copy and pasted, match for fucking match. They'll destroy each other before either one comes out the winner and here are my other two watching with bloodlust in their eyes and smiles on their faces. They are enjoying watching these guys kill each other and in any other circumstance, I'd likely be right there with them. The adrenaline rush and endorphin boost I get from even just watching a fight is an intoxicating addiction.

I'm zoned in on the fight, awe struck at the beauty and grace they both display when Matteo glances my way and winks. Ren sees it and looks to me as well, only to end up on the wrong side of 'Teo's foot connecting with his chest and knocking him on his ass. Ren wastes no time jumping back onto his feet and rushing his brother.

They are a tornado of bodies flipping each other over with arms, elbows and fists flying free. Shirts are getting ripped during the rough grappling and blood is flowing, making a mess all over the mats. I'm stunned at first; frozen solid in a state of shock and lust, but it doesn't take long for me to snap out of it and rush to them, only to get yanked back from behind. A strong arm wraps around my waist and a voice sounds at my ear.

"Not yet, Q. Let Noah's giant ass separate them first. They won't even see you and I'm not risking you getting hurt, even if you are the biggest badass I know." I feel the whisper of Cohen's breath waft over my skin, causing those stupid fucking goosebumps. Now is not the time to be affected by these assholes. I'm already struggling with my hormones left and right from all this fighting.

Noah is quick to reach them, grabbing Ren by the back of his shirt and yanking him up. Noah is one of the biggest men I've ever seen in my life, but Ren's entire presence makes him a viable match physically and when he spins around turning his anger on Noah, he clips him in the jaw hard enough that a lesser man would've been knocked out cold. Not my pretty boy though. The batshit crazy motherfucker turns a bloody smile at me and winks. God, I love him, the psycho fuck.

"Stop!" I yell. I'm fucking fuming in the place that Cohen is holding me back, trying to ground me with soft coos and loving statements. I'm too pissed to hear any of it though. My whole body is vibrating with rage as it courses through my body, head to fucking toe.

"Matteo. You and me… Right. Fucking. Now. You want a fight? I'll give you one. You wanna get dirty. Let's fucking go. Ren isn't the problem. *I* am. I made the final call on welcoming him into my life and therefore, into all of our lives. I thought you'd understand, given what you've been through with your dad and the shit you know to be true about our pasts. I know this isn't easy, but I already gave you an out once. You chose to stay. You chose to fight for me. Now you're going to actually fight me until you pull your head out of your ass and realize that the real enemy isn't your brother."

I don't realize that Cohen let me move closer to him, until I'm directly in front of him, shoving at him. I'd love to knock him on his ass right now, but even after an honest to Poseidon, knock down drag out fight, he's still got his center of balance and he hardly budges when I push him.

He lets me throw punches and kicks, not bothering to do any more than block my attacks.

"Fight back!"

He's giving me nothing in return, not bothering to say anything or fight back, he just keeps blocking everything I throw at him.

Feeling at my wits end with his "fuck off" stare and lack of response, I back away from him and turn to walk away, leaving all the boys to glare at each other like big ass children.

I'm not going to keep wasting my breath. If he wants space, I'll have to give it to him. I'm not a mind reader and I have no idea how to bring them together.

Unless...

Ah fuck, I'm an evil genius. Why I didn't think of this before is the real question. This is gonna be *good*.

Slowly, I start to strip off my spandos and sports bra, glad I didn't bother putting anything else on. Once I'm naked, I fake cough loud enough to catch the attention of the guys and then turn to walk away again. I don't even make it to the lockers before I'm turned around and hoisted up onto Noah's waist. He turns us back around and leads us to the mats, his eyes filled with lust.

"Uh, uh, uh, my feisty girl. You know better than to wave that sexy ass around and not expect me or the guys to jump you. We've been missing your fine as fuck self for too long. Plus, I think we owe you a punishment or two if I remember correctly." He speaks into my neck, causing shivers to race up my spine while he puts me down on my feet. I feel Cohen at my back just as my feet touch the ground and he buries his face into the other side of my neck.

"Fuck baby, I don't know exactly what your plan is here, but it's working. Those two aren't at a standoff anymore because they can't take their eyes off of you. Hell, none of us can. You are a fucking savage beauty."

SIXTEEN

ALESSANDRA

I'M in sexy man sandwich heaven when they start kissing and sucking on my neck, ears, shoulders and collar bone. My whole body lights up with excitement and I don't even feel the soreness between my legs that I fell asleep with last night. My cunt is already spasming in lust for these guys and I can feel myself dripping with desire.

I sense their presence before I see them. I can feel the heavy weight of their stares and when I finally look up, it's a heady feeling to have both sets of piercing green eyes focused on me in such a lusty state. Just knowing they're watching me get worked up by Noah and Cohen turns me on unlike anything I've ever experienced. These boys sure know exactly how to push me past all of my limits.

"Strip. All of you. You may not like each other, but each of you is in love with me and I want all of you. Right. Now. There's nothing stopping us anymore and I *need* you." I breathe out my words in short panting breaths, unable to hide the longing in my voice. And surprisingly, they all listen. I'm practically drunk on lust and power. These boys sure do know how to worship their queen.

Noah lays me down on the mats and gives me no time to think about anything else before he goes down on me. He wastes no time with his normal teasing. His tongue dances along my clit rapidly and then just as he enters me with his finger, he bites down gently before licking his way further down, pulling his finger out of me and dragging my juices from my pussy down to my ass. He plunges his tongue inside of me at the same moment he inserts a finger into my ass and I stiffen at the intrusion, but my body quickly relaxes when the pleasure takes over once more. His mouth moves to my inner thighs; sucking, biting and marking me as his. The dominance in that move causing me to come. Hard.

"Ahhh, Pretty... Boy..." I barely get words out before they all get swallowed by Cohen's sweet mouth. His kiss searing my soul. God, I've missed this. I've missed *them*. He pulls back and drops down to suck my left nipple into his mouth.

"Fuuuucccckk..." I can't express how good it feels in that moment when Cohen prolongs my orgasm with his tongue and teeth on my breasts.

"Do you think you're finally ready for us? We won't go easy on you this time around." I hear Matteo's voice, but it feels far away and dreamy while I'm coming down from the high of my release.

"Do your worst, Your Majesty." I smirk.

My eyes are closed and I'm literally laying on the floor like gumby. I'm so relaxed, I don't even flinch when I feel him line himself up at my entrance. He thrusts the head of his cock into me, until he's fully seated and lets out a primal groan. It stings a little as my body stretches and adjusts to his size, but it doesn't take long before my body moves on its own against him.

"Mmm, my little queen likes to take control here too, huh?" He smiles down at me, amusement coloring his features before his look turns dark and serious, like I'm used to. He halts my movements by dropping his full weight down onto me and grinds himself ruthlessly into my body. He gets down into my face, so close our lips are touching, but he doesn't kiss me.

"You haven't earned the right to fuck me. You allowed him to take what was mine, so now I'll take the rest." He breathes the dark words onto my lips, his voice so low that I'd think I imagined them had it not been for the possessive gleam in his eyes. He kisses me fast and hard, before he rips his lips from mine, it's a punishment. It wasn't a kiss of the man I know who loves me. It was the kiss of a man who's irrevocably broken from what I've done. Everything he does is meant to dominate me and take away my control, my power. He needs to hurt me right now.

He pulls out of me abruptly and flips me over on the mats at lightning speed. He's so fast, I don't even have time to fight it. I feel the caress of his hands tracing the curves of my ass before the smack comes down hard and fast. Once, twice, three times... and then he grabs me by the hips with bruising force with one hand to pull my ass towards him, while shoving my upper body down onto the floor with his other hand between my shoulder blades. My cheek gets smashed into the mats and I look up just in time to see immense anger overtaking Ren. It radiates off of him and his whole persona becomes larger than life when he's mad. I can see him twitching to come to me and love me twice as hard for the pain his brother inflicts. He stops his movements when I mouth to him not to just yet. 'Teo needs this. I need this. I deserve this for the damage I've inflicted on his heart.

"Ti amo" I mouth to him. Comforting him as best I can through this. My need to protect both of their hearts right now, overtaking my good sense.

Next thing I know, Matteo is working his dick into my ass, using only my cum as lubrication. It hurts, I won't lie. My body is being held down by Matteo still, so I can't even attempt to adjust and find any comfort. My muscles hurt from the cramped position 'Teo has me in, but I'll endure this for him. I want to. Thrust after thrust, he pushes beyond the tight ring of muscle finally fully seating himself inside of me. When he moans my name I allow myself to relax a little bit.

"Fuck baby, yessss... Alessandra, how do you feel so fucking good?" He questions and then releases the hold he has on me, falling deeper into the pleasure he's getting from my body. In doing so, he's also bringing me a level of comfort I doubt he means to, allowing me to further relax against him and finally enjoy what he's doing. He reaches around and flicks my clit and it's just enough to stimulate me into an earth shattering orgasm, but he holds a steady rhythm and pushes me through it thrust after thrust, as if he's nowhere near done.

Ren loses the last of his control over the restraint he's shown while watching his brother take me and push me with the delicious pain he inflicts and the pleasure he draws from my body. I watch him make his way to me, eager to show his dominance as well. If I didn't know any better, I'd say he looks jealous. In fact, he does. He's beyond furious, which is to be expected from my possessive alpha mafia king, but to allow me to see the hint of insecurity shine through his mask is telling, considering we're surrounded by my other alpha male boyfriends. He needs this as much as Matteo does.

Matteo moans loudly from behind me and I get momentarily pulled away from the intense gaze of his brother, but when I turn back, I find his erect dick bobbing directly in front of my face, causing my mouth to water as pleasure rolls over me once again. I push myself up to my hands and knees before reaching up to grab him and squeeze the base of his cock and then roughly stroke him, mesmerized as I watch the precum leak from his tip. I can't help myself when I lean forward and lick it up, then swallow as much of his length as possible. I feel him at the back of my throat when he grabs my ponytail and wraps my hair around his fist and takes full control. At this point, I'm just being used by both brothers and whether they know it or not, they work seamlessly as a team. They are both rough as hell and I'm loving it more than I should. Have I mentioned I'm a sick bitch?

They work in tandem as they take me and it is doing all the right things to my heart. I never in life, thought I'd be okay with one guy taking advantage of my body, but as these two work their aggression towards each other out on me, I'm reaping all the benefits of it and loving every god damn second.

Their grunts and moans continue as they duel it out, racing each other to the finish line, when I feel my other two boys join the party again. One of them reaches down to play with my pussy, rubbing my clit to help get me off again, while the other, lays down below me and draws their tongue around my nipples and massaging my breasts.

"Mmmmm" I moan around Ren's dick, causing him to grunt in pleasure.

"Fuck, I need that pussy." Ren says and then he actually has big enough balls to push 'Teo off of me so he can change my position.

"What the hell, man?" Matteo fumes, glaring at Ren pulling me from the other three in one possessive move.

"Il mio re, you can't do this. We talked about this. You promised me you'd try."

"fanculo la mia vita." He growls to himself. Then he lays down and pulls me on top of him, giving the boys full access to the rest of me. I lean down and whisper.

"No, not 'fuck your life'. Fuck your woman. Own my body like you own my heart."

"You got it, mi amore. You asked for this." And fuck me, he does. My pussy squeezes the life out of his cock as I come hard all over him.

Not a minute later and I feel my guys surround us and Matteo adjusts my position again so he can push his dick back into my ass. He's pissed as fuck still and doesn't go easy on me, but it only sends me on a tailspin into another hardcore orgasm, my body clenching tight around both of them. My body is going to give out on me if these guys don't come soon. They once again find their rhythm together when Cohen and Noah move to be on either side of me.

Not wanting them to be left out, I reach out and grab them with both hands and help them stroke themselves. I do my best, stroking the length of their dicks to the tempo of the guys fucking the life out of me, alternating between the two of them with my mouth. I feel like a wild animal, losing all of my inhibitions and fucking all these guys at the same time. When they all come, it's explosive, brutal and messy. It is everything I never knew I wanted. It's something I couldn't have expected I would need.

This is just the beginning of these guys working together as a team. They may not fully realize it yet, but I can see how amazing this will be. Let's just hope I don't fuck it up again. With the secrets I'm still keeping, I'll be lucky if it doesn't all blow up in my face, so for now I'll just enjoy what we have together.

SEVENTEEN

ALESSANDRA

IT'S the fourth of July today. I likely wouldn't have even known that had it not been for the large shipments of fireworks that were delivered to the island and the crew of carefully selected workers that showed up to set up for the show Ren is having for us. I've just been doing my best to make the most of the time I've got with my guys during our summer vacation.

We've made it through a lot of ups and downs over the last month or so, and for the most part everyone is getting along. At least Noah and Cohen are getting along with everyone. They've made the biggest effort to legitimately get to know Ren, even though I hurt them with my actions as well.

Matteo and Ren are still struggling the most. If you didn't know them and they didn't have the same damn face you wouldn't assume they were brothers because they refuse to even attempt to build that relationship. How they act towards one another isn't like brothers, but more like disgruntled co-workers who are forced to be on the same team. I can't say they aren't trying at all, though. They are both at least making *some* attempt to make it work for me; it's just the absolute minimal effort possible.

It's a little scary how alike they are at times, stubbornness included. If they could both just pull their heads out of their asses, we wouldn't have a problem. But they can't see past their own ego at the moment, so we'll keep tackling things little bits at a time.

Though I've remained intimate with all of them, we haven't had everyone involved in those hot and heated sexy times since the gym. It's a little disappointing because that was probably the only time I've seen them all come together willingly to do something. Not to mention the stupid amount of satisfaction I got from it.

I'm stuck in my own daydreams of the hedonistic acts when I feel lips at my neck, a seductive citrusy scent and Matteo's gravelly voice in my ear.

"You need to get ready for dinner tonight, baby. The boys and I have planned a big dinner and show for you.. We have a special surprise for you."

"Okay, I can make that happen. Can I ask you something first?" I turn to look him in the eyes. He's the one I've been worried most about. He's the one who's kept his walls up the strongest. Fortified them more if that's even possible. He's certainly the one who's been caught the most off guard and had to adjust his perspective in the biggest way. He's sharing me with a brother he didn't know he had. That's got to be something he never saw coming.

"You can ask me anything. You can always talk to me. I'm sorry I've made you doubt that since I got you back. I know I've been a nightmare to deal with. I'm not exactly the best at dealing with my feelings. I'm better at choking them down."

"Are you kidding me? 'Teo, do you remember how hard it was for us to start *our* relationship because I'm such a stubborn bitch? This is all my fault. I really handled things so badly. I should've at least warned you or something about Ren-"

"Stop. If you had warned me that you'd fallen for another guy, let alone my brother - my fucking twin... I wouldn't have even come. I would've gotten in my own way and let go of the best thing to ever happen to me out of petty jealousy. Ren doesn't change things for me when it comes to you. Sure, we have a lot to work through before we're all one big happy family, but that's our beef and we'll work it out. There is never going to be a moment of my existence when I don't love you Alessandra. I need you like I need air to breathe. We all do.

"Now that I understand things, I can admit that I understand why this all happened the way it has, and why Ren thinks the way he does. I may not like it, but I sure as shit understand it. I'm willing to deal with it, as long as I get to keep you in my life. One day, you'll be my wife. That's not going to change either. I'm so fucking proud of you for allowing yourself to grow and handle all of this with the strength you have. You are still every bit the fierce woman I first met; only now you've learned how to open your heart and accept happiness. I'm just thankful you've looked beyond the jaded mindset you were so locked into and have allowed yourself to trust your journey. You're lighting the way for us all through this darkness. Can't you see that?" He looks down at me with raw honesty shining through his gaze and I've never been so thankful for the men I've been blessed with, which only makes the guilt naw at my gut even more than usual. I should be spilling the last of my secrets, but it wouldn't be fair to the other guys to do it without them here. Or at least, that's what I'm telling myself to buy some extra time.

I reach up and wrap my arms around his neck, pulling his face down to meet mine in a passionate kiss, enjoying the intimacy of this moment. I just wish I could make it last forever.

"Um, excuse *me*, bitch! How about a little love for your real main squeeze?! We know all these boys are just a sexy placeholder for the real deal... You know... *me*? We all know the truth!" SB yells at me from the doorway to the living room.

"What the- Oomph!" I get tackle-hugged by my best friend and we almost both fall on our asses. I've never been so excited to see another female in my life, though, so I'm not even mad about it.

"What are you doing here?" I ask without letting go of the death grip I've got her in.

"Dude, I freaking missed you. Did you forget that we were supposed to spend all summer together getting ready for our senior year? Senior year! It's the big one that's coming up, in just a couple months, don't act like you've forgotten. Puh-lease! This is our time bitch and you know it. No one was going to keep you away from me. Even if he *is* a super sexy, brooding bad boy, beast of a man." She wiggles her eyebrows provocatively at me.

I'm laughing so hard; I have tears running down my face and I can hardly breathe. Is this girl for real? Damn, I can't believe how much I've missed her.

"How'd you know where to come? How'd you get here? God, I am so fucking stoked that you're really here. A bitch can only take so much testosterone." I wink at her.

"Yeah, uh huh... I'm so sure it was such a hardship getting dicked down by four hot dudes. Like three wasn't enough. Cry me a river princess." She mimes crying and we both crack up, leaving Matteo to look at us like the total loons we are when we're together.

"I came here with your mom and grandpa. Ren actually brought us out here to spend time with you, though I have a feeling it was a group decision. I'll stay way longer than I'm welcome of course, but I think your mom and grandfather are only here for the week."

"Did you know this?" I swing my eyes to mister tall, dark and broody only to get a smirk and a nod in response.

"Where are they?" I ask, thrilled that I'm finally able to see my family. I need a dose of home. The guys have helped so much, but there's something about having the last three members of my family here that makes everything feel like it might be alright again.

"C'mon boo, let's go on a mommy hunt. I know she's ready to see you and actually see with her own eyes that you're unharmed and okay with the whole kidnapping thing. I'm pretty sure your gramps is in Ren's office with him reading him the riot act. To be honest, I'd steer clear of that room. Both of those men are dan-ger-ous with a capital D. That's a big fat no fucking thank you to being a fly on that wall."

Oh fuck, none of that can be good. I wonder how much Ren has told nonno...

"Sweet girl! Oh my god, look at you. You're glowing! Kidnapped and falls for her kidnapper? Your whole life is like a crazy story. I couldn't write something this crazy. Are you sure this is what you want?" Mom looks deep into my eyes to judge my sanity. Admittedly, she has a valid point. My life is honest to god a shit show, but I'm working with what I've got and I'm cool with it seeing as how I get four hot alpha males that worship the ground I walk on. Plus, you know, I love them. Even if that isn't what I ever expected.

"I'm good, mom. The beginning was a little rocky and I have to totally overlook the fact that I was basically sold like property, but just like with the guys, I don't think I really had a choice in the matter with Ren. My heart knew before the rest of me did. Plus, I have plans for Lorenzo. Did nonno put the hit out?"

"You'll have to ask him. You know I try to stay out of 'the business' as often as possible. La famiglia is not my thing unless you need me." She grimaces and lets out an involuntary shudder. I know how much she hates this life. All she's ever wanted was for us to be free of it. I know she hates my involvement more than anything, but at the same time, she understands that it's just a part of who I am. It's like I was created for this life.

"I'll tell you right now though, if I get my hands on Lorenzo DeLuca before anyone else, he'll wish he'd been taken out by someone who just wanted to make a quick buck and doesn't care if he's tortured or not. I'll take his punishment from his flesh myself for hurting our family and fucking with my daughter. Just because I hate this world doesn't mean I don't know how to handle... business." She smirks, but it's an evil kind of smile. I know she can be a badass. I know how protective I feel over my family and the boys. I know my mother's love is unwavering and fierce. I can't imagine being on the receiving end of someone who tried to fuck with her baby... again.

"Ahh, la mia luce! Come, come give your old nonno a hug, nipotina! I've missed you." I turn to see nonno posted up in the doorway with a warm smile and his arms wide open and my whole heart finally feels full. I have my family here with me now and I remember what I've been fighting for this whole time. I know Ren's grandfather has his own ideas, but I'm about to fuck them all up with a smile on my face.

"Nonno, I've missed you so much. I hope you didn't hurt Ren too badly during your meeting." I smile up at him from our hug.

"Ugh, I hope you really hurt that asshole." Matteo huffs out, earning him a glare from me and a big laugh from nonno.

"He'll live. He explained things a bit more in detail for me and I have an idea that his grandfather is in for a rude awakening with you coming into your own on the East Coast as well as at home." He smirks.

"I've met the head of the Gavino family a few times throughout the years, and I have no doubt you're itching to put him in his place. Do not underestimate him though, mia luce. He's known for his callous ruthlessness for a reason and Ren's reputation is just as... disturbing. Although, I have a feeling the womanizing ways of the past aren't quite Ren's style." He winks at me and I do my best not to laugh at his summary of the Gavino family.

"Well, you're not wrong. That old man is gross. Ren has had his moments. You can tell he's used to being in charge, but he's never made me feel anything other than respected. He's even come around enough that he's been ok with my relationships with the other guys... C'mon, let's hit the dining room. It's probably close to dinner time by now and I want you all to tell me everything that's been going on since I've been here. I'm sorry I couldn't reach you sooner. I've missed you all and I'm freaking stoked you came out here. Can we just focus on having a good time tonight, enjoy food, fireworks and family? Tomorrow we'll talk business, yeah?" I ask nonno.

"I'm just happy to see you're alright. I was angry when you went off grid, but I knew it was a possibility. Had you been gone much longer though and there would've been a wake of bodies trailing the United States in search of you. No one kidnaps you again, do you understand mia luce? We bury anyone else who tries. As it stands, I feel I am owed and so is your mother for the way things were handled. I'm so proud of how you've dealt with all of this. Especially when it came to Raffaele. I imagine you wanted to take out a hit as soon as you met the cranky old bastard. Just make sure to let me know if his grandson needs to be put in his place. As it stands, I've already had words with him about how he handled things. There's at least one life to be owed for the years we've lost with you and I intend to see it happen. Though tonight is about family. Tomorrow we'll figure out how to deal with those we call our enemies."

EIGHTEEN

ALESSANDRA

I CAN'T REMEMBER a time that I felt this blissful or fulfilled. I'm not sure if I could even explain how I really feel if I tried. It's like my soul has finally found peace. I mean, I know there's a darkness I'll always hold onto somewhere deep inside of me. You don't grow up in the slums with a crackwhore for a mother, fighting on the streets to stay alive and not have baggage, but I've finally learned to let go a little. Plus, I am living in a mafia world and I am a mafia girl. No- a mafia *queen*. Each of my guys is the next up and coming Don in their territories. They will forever be my kings and I am still sometimes a little shocked they are all mine.

Technically Matteo isn't meant to be more than an underboss unless I die, because I'm technically next in line after my grandfa- ther- fingers crossed he continues to live a long and healthy life, but I'm hopeful to talk to nonno tomorrow about making the necessary changes to switch that around. That spot is rightfully Matteo's. Not only has he grown up dedicated to living under the oath of Omerta. His blood has long since been spilled, even from a young age, to devote his loyalty to la famiglia.

The more I've learned about my history and grown into this

world, the more I want the rightful title to be given to him. I won't really be giving up any power in doing so, even if it seems like I am. I just hope nonno will go for it. I'll have to convince him that I'm the heart and soul of all of these men and they will work with me regardless of what title I hold. Therefore, I'll be the heart and soul of the mob and without the steady beat of the heart, there can be no life. Without a soul, there can be no redemption. This life isn't always clean, but it doesn't have to be pure evil. I can make things better. We all can. Together. Weird concept, but it's what makes us all strong.

We just work really well as a team and I trust all of them. Plus, contractually, nothing changes. The plan we originally made should work perfectly; we all come together and expand the territories by combining all of the families. Only now, Ren will need to be involved. There may be some difficulties in the way - it's almost guaranteed when dealing with the Gavino family, but nonno will know what to do with Raffaele and his guys. I'd be surprised if he weren't already planning a war on my behalf as it is.

I know he's holding back from how angry he really is. He knows that I've accepted things to an extent with Ren and how we're moving forward. Had I shown even the slightest hint of discomfort, this whole island and half of the east coast would run red with the blood of anyone who'd dared to go against Alessandro Salvatore when I went missing.

I'm not completely oblivious to the things he had done in my honor when I was found the first time. There was blood. There was gore. There was torture and pain and misery for anyone involved. Lorenzo was the only one who got away, the fucking bastard. He'll get what's coming to him though. It's only a matter of time.

The only times I can think of that I've come close to this intense state of contentment was when my mom and I had breakthroughs in our relationship, or I've gotten girl time with SB and learned what true friendship feels like, or learning about la famiglia with nonno and getting in quality time at the shooting range. Those intimate moments I've had with the guys, yeah, they've been amazing and perfect in their own right, but nothing can touch this moment right here.

I'm enjoying my first Fourth of July fireworks show ever on a private island that I've just found out was bought for me. It was apparently one of Ren's first big purchases. In a true-to-him fashion, he bought it thinking it would be ours one day. Little did he know that we'd be able to enjoy it as one big happy family. It's not far off the East coast so he can handle his business affairs easily and go back quickly if necessary.

I'm sitting in Cohen's lap in front of a fire pit roasting vegan marshmallows -weird yet delicious- surrounded by the rest of my family and listening to the easy flow of conversation and laughter. It's everything I never really knew I wanted. Even the twins are getting along.

When I planned out my future and set goals to get out of the hell I was living every day, none of this ever came to mind. I wanted something simple and while I expected to work hard, in fact I did work hard, I had tempered expectations. Nothing fancy, just attainable. It was always - get the best education I could. Get scholarships if possible. Get the hell out of Dodge. I wanted to build a comfortable and sustainable life for myself. I didn't even care if I was still considered "poor". I just wanted a diploma and the potential for college and a stable job- something moderately enjoyable if possible. I would've accepted damn near anything though, as long as it was away from the life I was living.

I didn't even see relationships in my future. I've never, not once, wanted to date. I never even so much as reacted to a guy until I laid eyes on Matteo that first time. Sure, I noticed when people were attractive, but I never got that heart pounding, sweat inducing, mouth drying, hard to breathe feeling around anyone. No tingles. No frayed nerves or damp panties. Nothing that I feel with each of these guys. Even now after months, you'd think I'd feel less like an emotional pile of hormones, yet here we are and I wouldn't change a thing.

"Can you creeps back off? And maybe wipe the drool. Y'all act like you've never seen her before, but you've already had her for, like, half the summer. I'm her best bitch, not you. I'm claiming some time. Go on, shoo!" SB actually makes a shoo-ing motion that has me internally dying to crack up. Watching my little five foot some odd inches best friend push my four giants out the door is hilarious.

"Hey!! Michelangelo, Donatello, Leonardo and Raphael, are you listening to me? Go eat your pizza and practice your ass kicking skills or whatever you do to prepare to fight the bad guys... or are *you* the bad guys and I'm giving you too much credit? Whatever, it doesn't matter. Go. Away. Girl time! That means you punks gotta get gone." She bosses my guys around like they are small children instead of the giant beast monsters they are. These guys are literally some people's worst nightmares and she's acting like they're just an easy nuisance to take care of. They may as well be nothing more than flies in her sweet tea. She's a bad bitch, no doubt, because even some grown ass men wouldn't dare take them on. They all grumble as they listen to her and leave, but not before each of them gives me a heart stopping kiss and gets their fill of handfuls of ass. Even still, not many people can do what she just did and I'm impressed. It's a real party trick.

"What do you want to do today that you need them all gone for? You're being pushy, even for you. Ha." I grin at her to take some of the sting out of my words. She *is* being pushy, but not really in a bad way. I've missed her sass.

"Am I not allowed to have a day with my favorite girl? Nope, not listening to that bullshit. I haven't seen you in forever. I won't lie, when you went missing again, I really started to worry. You kept all of this secret message stuff to yourself and then just took off to take it all on yourself. It was pretty selfish of you and I was just as pissed off as I was scared." She looks down, unable to look me in the eyes. She's genuinely upset, so I grab her hand and hold tight while she tells me what she clearly needs to get off her chest.

"Hey Steph, you know I never meant to hurt you or scare you, right? I fucked everything up with the way I handled shit, but I wouldn't have done it if I thought for a second, things would've gone down like that." I try to offer her whatever comfort I can. I know I'm doing a shit job though, because she still can't even look at me let alone acknowledge I spoke.

"I mean, don't get me wrong. I know that what you did was far more selfless than actually selfish, but without knowing what we all know now, it didn't feel like that at first. Ya, know? It was like you just up and disappeared on all of us. You really hurt everyone and while I'm sure the guys haven't gone into a whole lot of detail about how they were after Matteo watched you get kidnapped, well, it was really fucking ugly." Her face scrunches up, like she's uncomfortable with even the memory of their anguish. She really cares about them. If I didn't know better, I'd almost feel jealous at how much she seems to care for each of them.

"I don't know if any of them even slept. Matteo went on a tear looking for his dad. He left a wake of destruction behind him everywhere he went. He took on some of his dad's biggest confidantes and broke them all before handing them over to your grandfather. Noah hit the underground cage fights every night and was rumored to have even killed a couple of guys trying to let out some of his aggression. Cohen and I teamed up to do a lot of the investigative computer work and create a paper trail. I think he knew more than he let on about the Gavino family. In fact, I'm pretty sure he figured everything out, but was waiting to confirm it before telling any of us the truth. He was getting close to learning something when his watch alerted him of your tracking device." She finally looks at me, giving me the smallest indication that she's not still fully upset with me.

"I've never seen him so happy, honestly. They all jumped into action so fast, I almost got whiplash. I felt pretty guilty that I'd already spoken to you at that point, so I think they knew something was different with me. I'm not exactly a great actress." She huffs out a laugh, and I laugh with her.

"You? You're not the best actress? How is that possible? You're the most dramatic person I know. Every day with you is like living day in and day out theatrics." I smirk at her, letting the laughter touch my eyes so she knows I'm just kidding.

"You going missing actually got me thinking about a program I'd like to create. I actually started developing at the beginning of summer to keep track of you, you know, after I found you. I know you have your necklace, but I didn't know about it when I came up with the idea, and a necklace can obviously be taken away from you, so I'd like to find something a little more discreet. I'm still ironing out the details, but I wanted to know what you think about the idea." When she looks at me then, her lips curl into the most evil of smiles, as she lets out a horrifying giggle, one that rivals that of those creepy haunted dolls no one ever wants to come in contact with.

"Oooh! I've got it! How do you feel about getting a new piercing?" And just when I think her devious smile can't get more evil, she winks and I laugh until I cry.

NINETEEN

ALESSANDRA

THIS LAST MONTH has gone by in a blur. My mom and nonno were only supposed to be here for a week, but thankfully they extended it a little bit longer. Mom and I worked out and she reminded me how good she is on the mats. I got my ass handed to me a few times. Nonno being the boss worked in our favor because he just moved some meetings around and called it good. I'm perfectly happy with that.

We ironed out all of the details for the contracts involving me and the guys, plus the special "gift" for Matteo, and he even helped me come up with a plan to deal with Raffaele's misogynistic bullshit if, or more realistically when, it comes up again. For now, I'll play my part as the sweet little doting female to Ren in front of anyone outside my family and once everything is finalized with the other guys' contracts, I'll take Raffaele down a peg or five.

I'm not a total idiot. I know it'll be dangerous. He doesn't have the reputation he does because he's a little bitch and he sure as hell didn't get to be the boss by tiptoeing around big problems. I'm about to be his biggest problem, so there are some safeguards in place for that. Plus, I've stayed true to my word with Ren and kept him in the loop with everything since it's his grandfather I may or may not have to kill. None of my guys would let anything happen to me if they could avoid it, but there's still a lot 'Teo, Noah and Cohen don't know. I've wanted to clear the air with them since my heart to heart with SB, but I just can't find a way to lay everything out. So nonno and I kept a lot under wraps while we discussed everything and kept most of our business meetings to the office without everyone else present.

Eventually though they left and the guys, SB and I all spent the rest of the time relaxing and enjoying our mini vacation. Sunbathing, swimming, learning the ins and outs of the island, watching movies and playing games. It's been the most fun I think I've ever had. With summer winding down, I'm not really ready for it to be over. Which is weird because I've always loved school, or at least, I've loved learning and being driven towards a singular goal. That and summers growing up meant not having guaranteed meals and a way to escape the house for something slightly less dangerous.

Ren says that I don't have to go back to school. We technically can do everything from here and I was ahead of the curve for the most part so graduating isn't something I have to worry about not happening. Do I really want to give up my senior year though? Especially after the way things ended last year. I was sort of looking forward to walking the halls with my newly built family. It's the experience I don't want to miss out on, I guess. I'll have to make up my mind when the guys decide what they want to do. There isn't anything really stopping anyone from staying here. The twins are eighteen and one of them has already graduated. Cohen and Noah are both capable of doing their classes online. SB might have a slightly harder time convincing her parents, but I don't mind having a polite chat with them to get my way if necessary. It'll have to be a decision we make together as a whole.

I feel arms wrap around me, pulling me out of my self-reflective thoughts. I can smell a hint of aftershave just before Cohen drops his chin to my shoulder, wrapping me up so completely, I can't imagine wanting to be anywhere else. Our view is amazing since I was already gazing at the lazily setting sun. It's like it knows how beautiful it is, so it's prolonging it's time before it fully sets. Like somehow, the sun knows how much ugly I've seen in the world and has decided to give me something so beautiful and bright, it makes up for all the darkness I've endured.

"Hey Red, what's up?" I turn in his arms to see something even more phenomenal than the sunset. The love and affection shining back at me has me feeling dizzy, my body warms up all over in response. Fuck, I'm getting soft. One look from any one of these guys and I turn into mush. I wonder how long it'll last. Does true love really withstand the test of time? All those fairytales I refused to believe in might actually come in handy right about now.

"Just seeing what you're up to tonight. Do you think I could steal you away for a couple of hours? I found something today and I want to show you." He smirks at me, and I know whatever it is it's gonna be perfect.

"Where are we?" I ask.

We've been walking down the beach for some time now and we've had to hike a bit into the forested area behind the manor. I can still see it, but it's distant. Admittedly the hike has been easy and beautiful with the low setting sun behind us. It's mostly dark now, yet it's all easy going since we're walking a manmade path. It was pretty apparent once I saw the hidden walkway, but it's something you wouldn't know was there unless you already knew it existed or found it by accident.

Surprisingly, the farther you get away from the estate, the more lanterns glow along the trail. They look like fancy solar pan-eled ones, which for whatever reason makes me super happy. I hope

Ren was behind that, doing his part to keep things as eco-friendly as possible.

"It's just up here Q, sorry I'm making you walk so far, but I swear it's worth it. I brought all kinds of stuff for us to snack on too. I didn't mean to pull you away before dinner, I just don't want you to miss this before the sun fully sets."

"It's fine Red. I'm happy to spend time with you and the view on this walk has been too beautiful to complain about." I smile softly, letting him know I'm truly enjoying my time.

"You know, I'm the one who found everything at your old house after you left it. I saw the flowers and the notes and the dress. I found some old documents basically stating your ownership to one Lorenzo DeLuca Jr., to be Underboss of Chicago. I can't believe I was so stupid to overlook the fact that Matteo's grandfather wasn't Lorenzo Sr. I'd only ever heard of him, never met him and I just didn't put two and two together. I've never known that kind of fear. Don't get me wrong, I was furious as well, but when I got the call from Matteo saying you'd been taken, the fear that overcame me was practically paralyzing. It's like my brain just shut down and all I could see, think or feel was your absence." He drops his head, like he's ashamed, but why? He couldn't have predicted that we'd uncover all of Lorenzo's shady secrets in an instant.

"For someone who's always ten steps ahead, I sure fucked all that up. I sort of felt responsible that I hadn't seen anything from those few days coming and I should have. The documents I found really tripped me up, and then you were just gone. I took everything from your old house and when I finally got everything laid out in front of me again, I started to finally piece it all together. The fact that I couldn't find any records of a DeLuca *Junior* was really fucking with me, it didn't make sense unless Matteo had a sibling, but I didn't tell him because I wanted to verify everything first. I was working on getting sealed records unsealed and buried paperwork unburied when you tripped your alarm, so I dropped everything and ran, we all did, we just ran to you.

"The whole situation had screamed mob interference from the get go, I just had to dig a little deeper. I know I would've found you one way or the other, there wasn't an option not to. I knew you'd been sold like property to the Gavino family thanks to Lauren's secret stash of paperwork. It was only a matter of time before I found out Lorenzo Jr. and Ren Gavino are the same person and then I would've tracked him down and found you. Nothing could have stopped me." The sincerity in his tone allows notes of residual sadness and anger to touch his words and it's truly all my fault, I should've been honest with him - with all of them.

"Cohen... That's not true. You can't be expected to always know everything before it happens. You aren't a mind reader for fuck's sake. I'm the one who fucked everything up. I should've never left without talking to you guys first. I- fuck... I just- ugh, I just wanted to keep you all safe... I didn't think with logic, I just reacted. You guys are really making me soft. It's annoying." I faux glare at him, trying to lighten the mood a bit because I can't keep getting swept up in all these feelings. I think my brain is about to short-wire from all the girly emotional bullshit I've put it through these last several months.

"You? Soft? That's debatable. I don't think anyone that has their own harem of made men can be considered 'soft'. Ha." He turns a skeptical gaze on me.

"Oh my god, you really just said that out loud." My eyes widening in mock shock.

"I did. But really Q, you're not going soft just because you are finally allowing yourself to let go of the bullshit from your past and growing into the woman you were always meant to be. From day one, you've been a force to be reckoned with. Like, the most beautiful storm, only the lasting damage left behind was all internal. You were so closed off and forever fighting all your demons in the dark. Now you practically glow from within. Your fight hasn't gone away, but you're finally fighting for the right reasons. It's pretty insane to be one of the people watching it all happen." And I realize in this moment why it was so easy to fall in love with Cohen Beckett. No one has ever seen me the way he does. He's the perfect calm to my chaos. He puts me at ease like no one else.

"For what it's worth. I am sorry that everything happened the way it did. I never meant for you guys to get hurt. I can't say I'm sorry that Ren is involved though. It feels so seamless to be involved with him. I just wish it had all happened in a better way." I say but feel like I need to just tell him everything. It's not enough to just apologize for what he knows. He deserves the truth - they all do.

"Hey Red, I need to tell-"

"Q, calm down. It all worked out the way it was meant to, it's fine. All that shit is behind us. We're almost there now, so let's just enjoy our night together, yeah?"

"Yeah, okay…" I agree as we pull up to what looks like a twelve foot tall leafy curtain. It almost looks like ivy actually, it's lovely. I guess I should wait to tell them all together anyway.

When Cohen pulls the leaves aside, I see what he was so excited to show me and it takes my breath away. The trees open up to let the skies show above, and the pink hue in the sky from the sunset, reflects and sparkles off of the small waterfall straight ahead of me. The waterfall flows directly into the largest of what looks like three separate pools of crystal clear water.

Surrounding the pools are large stones that look as though they've been carved out by the water to make perfectly circular swimming holes. The largest pool sits in the middle, slightly higher off the ground then the other two, which allows the water to flow over into them.

There's a few of the surrounding rocks that look like they could be used to jump into the water if it's deep enough. The two pools on the side look much more shallow, the water so clear you can see all of the multi colored rocks at the bottom, but the large pool of water in the middle turns into a deep shade of midnight blue towards the middle and the closer you get to the back by the waterfall.

"You wanna take a dip? The water is surprisingly warm. I found this place earlier today and it's definitely a hidden paradise. Or we can eat if you want?"

"I'm not hungry yet, but I didn't bring a swimsuit." I can feel my face scrunching up, showing my displeasure without my consent. I am bummed though, I kind of want to explore that waterfall. I've never seen one in real life.

"Why would you need a swimsuit?" He winks and then starts stripping off all of his clothes, leaving me sex crazed and desperate for him to take it all off faster.

Ho-ly shitballs, the man is so fine. He's beefed up a little since being here on the island. Whatever workouts he and the guys are doing are really freaking working for them. Those abs are drool worthy on a good day, but that 'V' leading down to his very erect dick is doing all kinds of crazy things to me.

Instead of coming to help me remove my clothes, like he normally loves to do, he walks toward the largest pool and dives right in, giving me an equally pleasing view of his sculpted ass. No one should look that good while showing off such a milky white ass, and yet here we are, with me staring and hoping I haven't drooled all over myself.

TWENTY

ALESSANDRA

I'M STRIPPING my clothes off so fast; I'll be surprised if I don't find anything ripped when I come back to the careless pile I'm creating on top of Red's stuff. The need to be wherever Cohen went is consuming me completely, so I race my naked ass over to the three pools as fast as I can. I'm sure I'd look funny as shit to anyone actually looking, since I'm holding my boobs in place as I book it along the path leading to the water, but he's swimming toward the waterfall so luckily for me, he's missing the comedy show.

Not bothering to test the water, I dive right in, just like he did, only I swim farther than he originally did to get to him faster. When I come up for air though, he's missing. The water is too clear to miss him so I know he's not swimming underneath me, which only leaves behind the waterfall for him to hide.

I carefully swim over, looking for the weakest section of falling water so I can swim through it, or maybe under it. I take my chances and dive down as deep as I can, trying to make my own way through the water instead of just letting the current from the rushing water push me around.

By the time I come up for air, I'm pulled into the warmth of

Cohen's arms and I realize he's pulled me into a shallow section of water. So shallow I could stand if I wanted to, but I'm too content to sit in his arms and look at the cavern surrounding us. The small bit of light that shines through the water shows off the brilliance of the glittery minerals throughout the cave, making it appear as though we are surrounded by millions of stars. Everything he's shown me so far has meant so much more than just another romantic gesture. He's tapped into my need to see the world outside of the jaded life I've led. He's offering me the opportunity to experience something as normal as going on a date with my boyfriend and something as crazy as exploring hidden caves full of glittering stones and swimming in all natural waters, untouched by other people. He's giving me back my sense of adventure and wonder. It's a gift, I won't take for granted.

"Thank you so much for bringing me here. I'm not sure I can put into words how spectacular this whole experience is. I love you Red."

When I don't get a response, I turn my body around so that I'm straddling him and then pull his face into my hands, forcing him to look at me. Everything he's told me must feel really heavy for him to not allow himself to fully enjoy this moment with me. I'm just not sure he'll let me help him get out of his funk.

"Q, I don't deserve your love. I couldn't even keep you safe. The one thing I've always done better than others is think ahead. I've never met a puzzle I couldn't solve until this mess. I guess I'm having a harder time letting it go than I thought. I'm just worried I'm going to let you down again."

"Knock that shit off. I'm dead ass serious right now Cohen. What happened wasn't your fault. If anything, it was *my* fault. I walked willingly into the darkness to fight my demons. It's not your fault that you didn't have all the information. You practically had it all figured out anyway. No one else could've put everything together like you did. You used your pain from losing me to motivate you to do the extraordinary. To put it simply, you would've found me. I don't doubt that. Your heart will always find mine. Always. There were some moments after I got here that I genuinely felt like I could feel your pain. I know that sounds stupid..."

"No, it really doesn't. I don't think a single one of us didn't go through that in some way or another. It's like the world lost all its color without you in our arms. Nothing was good. Matteo internalized everything. I know he spent all his time looking for his dad and not eating or sleeping. We still need to find him, but now I feel like I sent him on a wild goose chase because I'm the one who told him it was Lorenzo. I didn't give him all the information... And Noah... Fuck, I'm not sure I even want to know everything he did. I know he went underground to find information about Lorenzo's location as well. If what's rumored is true, he made Harold Shipman look like a real nice dude. The underground streets are probably still stained red."

Instead of responding, I kiss him with every ounce of passion I have within me. The kiss is frantic and needy. It's all lips, teeth and tongue as I battle him for dominance. I want him - no I *need* him to feel how sorry I am for running away, how much I appreciate him for never giving up on me and how much love I have for him. I also want him to understand how desperately I want him.

I grind down on him, bringing back that erection from before and damn does it feel good. Every time I grind down, the tip of his cock hits my clit and sends my nerves into catastrophic bliss. He tries to end the kiss, and trail his mouth further down my body, but I'm not ready to be done with that mouth. I grab his chin and bring him right back to my lips.

"Never stop kissing me Red. Your lips taste like forgiveness and redemption." I whisper, barely touching my lips to his.

This time he initiates the kiss and there's not an ounce of thought left in my mind as I'm wholly consumed by him. His tongue wages a war against mine as he makes the kiss violent, releasing all his frustration into this kiss. When I bite his lip, I draw a small bit of blood and it sets him off with a groan.

He lines himself up at my entrance and pushes inside so slowly,

I'm practically ready to beg him to move harder and faster by the time he's fully seated inside of me. Instead of moving, he just stays there, content to be there while kissing the life out of me. He holds my hips in place so I can't move and the lack of friction between us is driving me mad.

My inner walls clamp down on him hard enough to make him moan, but he still won't move and my body thrums in anticipation. When his hands slide up and down over my hips, ribcage and back down to my ass, I take that as the go ahead to finally move and so I do, I start to ride him hard and fast, grinding down with a force that breaks apart our kiss and shoves my boobs into his face every time I move upward.

"Slow down my love, we have plenty of time to get there. Let me savor each second with you. Tonight I want to show you what it means for *me* to love you. Just relax, okay?"

He reaches up and grabs each of my breasts in his hands and alternates kisses between each handful, sucking my nipples into his mouth before biting down gently and sending shockwaves down my pulsing cunt, that alone almost has me coming.

Somehow he manages to make me feel like he's touching me everywhere. Between leaving bruising kisses all over my body to offer little bits of pain - serving to only heighten my pleasure, and his tender caresses across every inch of my skin he can get his hands on, and every deliberate thrust into my body, I feel like I'm nothing but sensation and bliss.

Bringing his forehead to mine, he looks me directly in the eyes while he makes love to me. It seems like a move that would be cringey because that should be weird, right? It's not, and I feel so connected to him in this moment that I can't help it when I come, screaming his name.

He pulses in and out of me with shallow thrusts while I come down from the high of my orgasms before he really starts moving. My nails claw into his back as I try to keep up with his brutal rhythm, or at least hold on for dear life as he uses my body however he sees fit.

This is the Cohen I very rarely get a glimpse of. The man that comes unleashed and takes full control. He is assertive and has no problem taking his pleasure from my body, but only after he's ensured I got mine first. The perfect dichotomy. My quiet, sweet, reserved lover turned domineering and savage. He's perfect.

After leaving bite marks all over my breasts and neck, he moves his mouth to my ear and whispers "come" at the same time he swirls a finger around my clit, and when my body gives into his command, his rhythm stutters and he comes deep inside of me at the same time.

He doesn't bother removing himself from me as my body gives way to the physical exhaustion one can only experience after mind blowing sex. Instead, letting me continue to drape myself over him and enjoy the afterglow in the warm waters of the cave.

TWENTY-ONE

ALESSANDRA

WHEN I WAKE UP, I'm wrapped around Noah with Cohen spooning me from behind. I almost feel like I should pinch myself, because this life I'm living has to be a fantasy.

My body is sore in all the right places, and while I'm paying for it today, I wouldn't have changed a thing about my date with Cohen last night. After he thoroughly fucked my brains out, we swam and ate, and laid out under the stars talking about nothing and everything before walking the semi long trek back to the estate. It was everything and I'm super thankful we were able to spend some time alone.

When we got back though, I had to promise Noah a date today and Matteo a date tomorrow. The giant man babies whined and cried until I caved. Ren just rolled his eyes and kissed me thoroughly enough to curl my damn toes. Then the sexy asshole winked at me and told me he'd be working through the next week so I wouldn't see him again for a while.

I saw the boats at the dock last night so I know he'd gotten on one to head back to New York to deal with his grandfather. I know he's an Underboss, but it seems as though Raffaele uses him as an enforcer as well. *Il Diavolo* - The Devil, I overheard him being called when I was in his office "helping" one day. I know he's killed men before, but it wasn't until that moment that I realized he's *the* Devil. As in, one of the most notorious, diabolical hidden treasures amongst the Italian mafia.

I should be terrified, but it honestly turned me on so much that I stripped out of all of my clothes and completely distracted him from work the rest of the day. Again, I'm fully aware that I'm a sick bitch. The blood on their hands only serves to make me wet.

It doesn't take away from how much I already miss him or how worried I'll be until he gets back. His day job is dangerous. The things he does in the dead of the night would give your nightmares, nightmares. There is no life or death in what he does, there is only death and whatever comes after.

I'm sure I should move, probably should get up and start the day. I can almost guarantee 'Teo is already up and working out, but I'm so content in my yummy naked sandwich that I decide to snuggle in a little deeper instead. It can't be later than mid-morning and SB sleeps in until like two everyday so she won't barge in here threatening anyone without clothes on until at least two thirty, because god forbid she lets anyone other than me see her crazy red curls turned bedhead.

The girl is as wild as her hair and stupidly attractive. This next year at school, I'll need to keep an eye out for her to start her own harem of hot dudes. If anyone deserves it, it's my best bitch. I love that whack job and want to see her as happy as I feel.

Because I'm a glutton for punishment, I start to grind my hips back into Red's morning wood, gaining his sleepy sighs as a reward. Wanting more voices added to my morning symphony, I reach my arms around Noah's waist, and get a tight grip on his morning erection pumping my hand up and down to the same tempo as my hips working my ass against Cohen,

"Wake up Pretty Boy. It's time for us to play." I sing-song a whisper into his neck, only to get a growl in response.

He moves his hand down and covers mine on his dick. Right

when I think he's going to stop me, he puts more pressure on my hand, causing me to squeeze him so hard, you'd think it'd hurt, but he just growls again and then moves his hand away to reach behind him and grab my leg to pull over his body from behind. While it pulls me away from rubbing myself all over Cohen's dick, it opens up my legs enough that with a small shift of bodies, Cohen has moved in and fucks me proper from behind.

I guess my wake up call for them worked. And now I get all the benefits from it.

"Both. I need you both... Please..." I beg, my voice rough from sleep, causing me to sound much more sultry than I ever have before. I don't even recognize myself.

Another quick change in our positions and I'm riding Noah's dick instead while Cohen grabs some lube out of the bedside drawer. I hear him squirt some into his hand and start rubbing it on himself, warming it up a little before he places himself against my ass. Pushing in slowly, he allows me to adjust to his size as he pushes past the tight ring of muscle, then matching his pace with Noah's. They work me over together until I'm a panting, sweating, tingling bundle of overstimulated nerves. With nothing more than a thin layer of skin between the two guys, I feel almost too full, but in the best way. It's so good. So, so fucking good.

"Yessss! Fuck. Shit. I'm coming. Guys, I'm coming!" I scream. Unable to hold back and uncaring of who may hear me, my body locks up and tightens around them both, pulsating with the tiny little aftershocks that seem to have taken over and worked their way through my body from head toe. Cohen comes first, stilling behind me and yelling out during his release. When he starts pulling out, Noah's body tightens up and he roars out his own release, not bothering to move my collapsed body off of him yet.

Cohen gives me a hard smack on my ass and then moves toward the bathroom, only for him to turn in the doorway to face us.

"C'mon you lazy bums. Shower. Breakfast. Gym. Let's move."

And with a wink, he steps fully into the bathroom, knowing we're not far behind.

"Good morning, Your Majesty! I missed you in bed last night." I say with a kiss for my broody bastard. Not even his cranky ass can ruin my good vibes today! This much sex has a way of ruining a girl in all the right ways.

"You didn't sound like you missed me. Last night or this morning. I've jacked off three times since last night to your beautiful sexy moans and screams. Thank god, it's a skeleton crew for the house staff right now. You'd likely scare the full staff away." He grumbles. So fucking cute when he gets jealous. Ugh, that should not be cute. What happened to the "I am woman, hear me roar." bitch I used to be? These assholes have me whipped. It's a whole ass problem. Or it would be if they weren't just as whipped as me.

"Don't pout, you can always snuggle into the dogpile at night."

"I'm good, but don't worry, I'll make it up to you on our date. I'm taking you off the island tomorrow. Ren is working out of New York this week, and I know you'll want to check on him so we'll make a day of sightseeing and being super touristy. Then we'll meet him for dinner before coming back to the island and then we're sleeping in Ren's bed. *Alone.*" His smile is almost cruel, if not for the blinding beauty accompanying the menace lurking in its depths. Goosebumps trail over my body and I shiver involuntarily.

My traitorous pussy, already greedy for more, is ready to start the date right this minute. Doesn't this bitch know that I already have a date with one of the cocks that literally just pounded the hell out of her? And why in the fuck am I thinking as if my vagina is its own entity? Hello crazy town, thank you for the warm welcome.

The dark chuckle that 'Teo lets out, does bad things to my mind, body and soul so I decide to walk away without responding.

"Looking forward to it my queen!!" He yells from behind me, and all I have left in me to offer him is my middle finger and a little extra sway in my hips, giving him a little something to think about while he's alone all day. The last thing I hear before I walk back upstairs is his laughter and it makes me happier than I'd like to admit.

TWENTY-TWO

ALESSANDRA

NOAH and I have spent the day doing a whole lot of nothing. We've listened to music and made each other playlists and sang each other cheesy love songs completely off key, just for the fuck of it.

We played in the ocean and stole some snorkel masks and one of the little blow up boats on the docks to go a little further out to see how many different kinds of fish we could find.

He told me stories about his childhood, which explains so much about him as the man he's grown up to be. Strong and fierce, unstoppable once he puts his mind to something. It doesn't matter if he's on a game field, fighting low life mobsters, or falling in love with someone just as damaged as he is. When he does something he gives it his all. Sometimes his all is bloody and messy and scary as fuck, but hey, no one's perfect and I love him even more for it.

His grandpa used to beat him bloody on the daily. His parents never stepped in to help. Thinking that it would make him stronger and work harder, they allowed a monster into their home to mold and shape my Pretty Boy in his image. What they didn't expect is for their monster to one day fight back and kill the man who tortured him since he was a young boy.

One day, he'll come for them too. They hold his title and his trust over him to keep him in line, but they had no problem shipping him off to boarding schools growing up and eventually to live with Matteo to finish out high school.

The dude is wicked smart, but only does enough schoolwork to keep up for sports. He's not convinced he needs an education when he's guaranteed a place in the family business and is basically only used as an enforcer as it is.

He's a lot like Ren in that way. Both of them hold their crazy in as best they can and unleash it when necessary. Ren wears his pain on his sleeve though, whereas Noah likes to hide his behind his perfect smiles and funny jokes and sexual capabilities.

Abuse is a senseless thing. It costs nothing to be kind and too many people take that for granted. What does it hurt to *not* say something horrible about someone or not bully a person. I'm not perfect, but I don't go out of my way to treat people like shit either. I would never treat anyone the way I was treated as a kid.

ABUSE SHAPES you in ways that you may never understand and it comes in so many forms; mental, physical, emotional... Some people might say because I wasn't beaten as a child, I wasn't abused by my fake mother. Some would argue that neglect is abuse in its own right and changed the course of my life immensely. I'd say, I turned it into the best situation I could and learned to fight for myself and my right to hold my head up high, walking with confidence in every step I take.

People are assholes and everyone has an opinion. It doesn't mean they are right. What happened to Noah isn't the same as what happened to me. But both could be argued that they've impacted us deeply regardless.

Noah arguably has the biggest heart of anyone I know. That heart wasn't treated with care when it should have been and yet he knows how to love with every bit of who he is. He's created a family between me, SB and the guys and I don't doubt for a second that he wouldn't kill for any one of us, that he wouldn't *die* for any one of us. He may be a monster, but he's the most selfless monster I know and I'm so grateful to call him mine.

"Whenever I get my period, I always feel like my cunt is more swollen, more desperate than usual…" Noah reads the line from my newly released book, a part of my new favorite book series out loud, *Chaos At Prescott High* by C.M. Stunich, and then turns to look at me, eyes widening the more he reads of the erotic, filthy scene. His dick is hard as a rock, and I'm swollen and wet. It's a good problem to have honestly. Maybe we should read to each other more.

"Is that true? Are you more horny when you're bleeding? We are *so* fucking getting it on the next time your period comes around." He gives me a suggestive smile, while offering up some crude sexual gestures, clearly designed to make me laugh. Guess what, it works. Childish humor works on me, huh. Interesting.

"Yeah, I mean. Sort of. I don't know if it's a hormonal thing or what, but I do tend to feel a little… extra around that time of the month. I'm down for whatever you want Pretty Boy. Don't you know I live to make you and the boys happy?" I smirk at him.

"I know you're kidding. I do, but between your words and this whole sex scene, I'm aching to fuck you. Right now. Bloody or not, I don't care as long as it's you I'm draining my balls into."

"Gee, you sure know how to make a girl wet, ya dick. Whatever happened to romance?"

"First of all, the romantic shit is more Matteo and Cohen's thing. I'm the fun one. Second, you're wet. I can practically smell your arousal from here and I can't wait to get a taste. And the third and final thing, arguably the most important thing; you are still owed a punishment for leaving me and pissing me off and I have every intention of getting what I'm owed." He says calmly, like he isn't calling me out and telling me he's going to punish me. What does the word punish mean in Noah's brain? Oh, fuck. I can't tell if I'm trembling in fear or excitement.

"Strip for me feisty girl. Let me see all of you." The gleam in his eye promised so much pain and so much pleasure, I can hardly do what he asks. Luckily, I'm only wearing a swimsuit and a cover from our outdoor adventures earlier today so I can get it done quickly and without too much thought.

"Now come lay that fine as hell ass down on this bed. Arms above your head." When I do as he says, I earn a genuine smile, causing me to want to please him more. Maybe there's something to this BDSM stuff after all. The more time I spend with these guys, the more I learn about my own sexuality. It's far more empowering than I'd ever thought it would be. He walks over to my dressers and pulls out... two pairs of panties?

When he brings the panties over to the bed I'm genuinely confused, that is until he uses each pair to tie my hands to the bed posts on either side of my headboard.

I test the bonds to see if they'll actually hold me, and sure as shit, they do. I don't know how I feel about this just yet, but if the wetness coating my thighs is any indication, I'm more excited than anything.

"Is it too tight love?"

"No, it's fine."

"Good. Now I'm going to flip you over so you're ass up, face down. Okay?"

"Uhh, sure. Mhm." I keep the tremble out of my voice, but only barely. I don't want him to think I'm afraid of him. Quite the opposite, in fact. I trust him more than anything, but my body is starting to show signs of desperation, including the shakiness of my voice.

"Damn, Feisty! This ass... Mmm, fuck. I could just..."

"Ow! What the fuck? Ha. Why did you bite me like that?" I try not to laugh, but I'm not doing a very good job apparently.

"Is something funny Feisty?" The dark note in his tone has me paying close attention to what happens next.

"Sorry, Pretty Boy. It just caught me off guard." I bite my lip and play coy. I know he can see right through me, but he's enjoying the game so he moves on.

"I'm going to spank you ten times and then I'm going to eat that soaked cunt of yours. It smells so good; I don't know if I have the patience to give you the spankings you deserve." He growls out the last part as if he's angry that he enjoys feasting on me when we both know that's far from the truth.

"Noah!" I can't help but yell when the first hit comes.

"Do you know why you're getting your ass spanked?" The second smack hurts, I won't lie, but when he runs his hand over the hand-print he's left behind, it feels like he's soothing it.

"You like it when I wear red?" I give him a smartass response, knowing he'll enjoy punishing me more for it.

"Alessandra. Don't piss me off right now."

Slap. Slap. Slap.

"Oh, I'm so sorry. I had no idea- Ugh." The sixth spank knocks the next smartass comment right out of me, along with my breath.

Slap. Slap. Slap.

"You left me. You kept secrets from me. You didn't trust me. You got yourself fucking kidnapped. I thought I lost you. I thought you were gone forever and the only light in my life was gone. The darkness consumed me until we found you again. I've never been so low. I'm not sure I could ever survive losing you again." And by the time the tenth smack lands, there's almost no force behind it.

"Untie me baby. Please." I let some real emotion resonate in my words, because I need to put our joking and smart ass bullshit away for a minute. I really hurt him. He's naturally the most easy going guy of the group, but that big front protects big feelings and I should've known better.

Grabbing him, I pull him up to me and cradle his face in my hands and wrap my legs around his lower body, holding him tight to me as best as I can.

"Noah, my love. I am so, so sorry for what I put you through. I never want us to go through that again. I- I don't want there to be secrets between us. There is something you guys don't know though. We all really should sit down together and talk."

"It's okay Alessandra. You don't need to spill all your secrets tonight. We'll all talk together if that's what you want. I'm just really fucked up in the head and I didn't exactly handle losing you very well. I shouldn't have taken it out on you like that. I do like spanking you, but that was too much."

"Nah, not too much. I'd take far worse if it meant you could heal a little bit. Don't you know there isn't anything I wouldn't do for you? I love you, you giant beast man. Even if you are the court jester." I wink at him and then pull him closer to snuggle him for a long while. And when we finally get back to the sexy parts of the night, he makes up for every smarting red mark on my ass with orgasms. Lots and lots of orgasms.

TWENTY-THREE

ALESSANDRA

THERE'S NOT enough caffeine on the planet for me to be okay with Matteo storming into the bedroom Noah and I played gymnastics in all night at six o'clock in the fucking morning, demanding I shower and get dressed for our day together.

There have been plenty of moments throughout our time together that I've wanted to hit 'Teo, yet never more than right now. Doesn't he know I was up all night playing tonsil hockey with my other hot as sin boyfriend?

Ugh, why is he such a prick? I know what it is, it's because he's always been the hottest dude around. It gave him a big head, which ultimately made him a bossy, rude ass mother fucker. I'm gonna hit him at some point today.

I push open the bathroom door, only to be hit in the face with steam and an eyeful of sculpted naked Matteo ass in the shower waiting for me. On the counter there's a glorious black and gold can of life essence in the form of caffeine. Maybe hitting is out and kissing is in. I guess there are worse ways to wake up. I'm just a bitch.

I down the energy drink real fast and make quick work of

jumping in the shower, wrapping my arms around the giant in front of me.

"Sorry, I'm a raging bitch monster. I shouldn't be an asshole when you've gone out of your way and planned a whole day for me." I smile into his back and trace the lines of his abs. He won't let me go further down, since he stops the descent of my hand.

"We've got to catch the first boat out today. Don't start something you can't finish my queen. It'd be too easy to slam you into that wall and get lost in you for the day instead."

"And you're sure we can't do that?" I pout.

"Not if you want to see Ren." He plays the one card I can't beat. I do want to see Ren. Surprisingly, even a couple of days without him feels wrong.

"Shit. Alright, okay. You win. Let's hurry up then. I can't be near a naked you and be expected to not act on it."

"Yeah, I can tell... Is that drool I see there?" He gives me a teasing smile, softening the dickish comment.

"Ha-fucking-ha dickbag. You aren't actually funny, ya know." I stick my tongue out, because when in doubt, go back to the classics. As in, pull out all the grade school tricks.

"Is that so?" He pushes me up against the wall, and my chest heaves out a breath I didn't know I was holding.

"Mhm."

"Well if not for humor, whatever else could I use my mouth for?" He smirks, knowing my sex crazed brain immediately comes up with several options for that pouty mouth.

I reach up on my tiptoes and give him a heated kiss. It's not slow and sensual. It's not angry or aggressive. But a fast burn kiss that takes you from zero to one hundred and the next thing I know Matteo has his dick deep inside me. We don't have time for anything than a hard, fast fuck, but it's enough to satiate us both because we come at the same time, with our lips still locked passionately a few minutes later.

"Okay, now let's go into the city! I wanna see everything." I smile and give him one more kiss, clean myself off real fast and go to get ready.

New York city is nothing short of spectacular. It's everything I ever imagined it was. We had breakfast at Tiffany's, well brunch but still. Matteo took me to see the Statue of Liberty and then we went to The National September Eleven Memorial and Museum.

We walked hand in hand through Central Park and got our portrait drawn, then went back through in a horse carriage. I ate at a hot dog truck, a falafel truck, an entire food truck designed to make all my dessert dreams come true. We each tried a Chik'n'Cone and shared another dessert from Serendipity's.

I got serenaded on the Subway, much to the dismay of Matteo, and I was proposed to by the Hulk in Times Square. The only thing missing is a night out on Broadway, but that'll have to wait because I'm really missing Ren. Today all of my NYC dreams came true thanks to Matteo and now he's putting his feelings toward his brother aside to give me peace of mind.

We walk into a quaint little Italian restaurant and Matteo moves us straight to the back. Everyone in the place stops and stares at us and it's beginning to feel a little too cliché. The Mob boss having a meeting at his own private table at a "family" establishment. Yada yada yada. Blech, I wish we weren't eating here.

"Mi amore!" Ren sees me and hugs me so tight; I can barely breathe. I accept it because he's okay. He's alive and well. I release a sigh of relief and send a silent thank you to whatever god is looking out for him.

"Matteo." Ren offers a polite nod to his brother and they both clasp my hands before they move us to the table.

"Ren, no offense, but doesn't this restaurant feel like too obvious a place to meet up?"

"What do you mean, mia bella?"

"Well, you know. Italian mafia boss. Back table. Spaghetti. I feel like I'm staring in a cheesy mob movie." I cringe, realizing I sound like an idiot.

When all I get are two deep sets of laughter echoed back at me, I get the feeling they think I'm joking, so we'll roll with that instead. At least they're getting along.

"So, how's work?" I ask, not expecting much detail.

"Work has been a mess. On top of having everyone out looking for Lorenzo, my right hand man, Piero got shot."

"Oh my god, is he alive?"

"Yeah, he's fine. It was a superficial injury at best. I don't take kindly to my people getting hurt though, especially Piero. He's practically family. So, I took care of it."

"You took care of what?"

"I took out everyone involved."

"How many?"

"Twenty-four."

"You took on twenty-four men? By yourself? Are you insane?!"

"Damn bro, that's fucking badass. Even I can admit that." Matteo nods his approval and I shift my glare between brothers.

"That's not badass. That's suicide. What the hell is wrong with you?" I'm so furious, I don't even realize I'm yelling until I feel a small hand on my shoulder.

"Oh, I'm quite angry as well, but maybe let's keep family matters away from our family table. Hmm?" The woman touching me damn near gets her head bit off, until I turn my fury on her only to immediately stare in shock. It's completely rude, I'm aware of that, but I can't help it when I look into the emerald green eyes of the twins' mother.

I pull myself together long enough to look at Matteo, making sure he's okay first and foremost. Other than the tightening around his eyes and noticing the tightening of his hand on mine, he gives nothing else.

Arianna on the other hand, can barely hold back the tears in her eyes as she gets a good look at her youngest boy.

"Uh, yes. I guess I should make the introductions then. Mamma this is Alessandra and Matteo. Everyone, this is my mother, Arianna Gavino. And just to clarify, I didn't take on all of those men at once. I was smart."

His mother and I scoff and roll our eyes at the same time, which somehow breaks the tension, causing everyone to laugh. Even Matteo.

"It's nice to finally meet you." 'Teo says.

"I wish it could've happened sooner. You'll never know how sorry I am that things happened the way that they did. For all of you." She looks around the table to ensure we understand her meaning.

"And Matteo, don't worry. I won't push. I know you had a mother. In fact, I'm truly sad that I can't thank her for raising such an accomplished young man. The little information I've been able to gather over the years tells me that she loved you and protected you like you were her own flesh and blood. I couldn't have asked for a better choice for you."

"Thank you. I appreciate that. It actually makes me feel surprisingly more comfortable with potentially getting to know you, knowing you respect her place in my heart. Even more so that you know where things stand with Alessandra."

"Okay, well what can I feed you all? Is Lasagna good for everyone? I've got a fresh batch coming out of the oven in five minutes." She rushes out and when we all nod our confirmation, she swiftly walks away, wiping her eyes as she goes. I think this could be the beginning of something really good.

TWENTY-FOUR

BY THE TIME we leave the boys' mom's restaurant, it's late. Ren had to head back to work so I let him go a few minutes ago, everything inside me screamed to hold him closer and not let him go. I just didn't feel right about him going back "to work" after his story. It put me on edge and I couldn't shake the bad feeling.

I kissed Ren within an inch of his life because I didn't really want to say goodbye, but I knew he couldn't get out of this. Raffaele Gavino doesn't accept call ins or sick days. So, I told him I love him and sent him on his way.

We stayed behind a few extra minutes, because once Arianna started asking Matteo questions, it didn't look as though she'd stop. Her excitement was palpable throughout the whole conversation and 'Teo did a really good job of keeping up with her questions.

I'd even venture to say that he enjoyed the onslaught of maternal love and affection she so naturally gave all of us. It's a true wonder that woman came from Raffaele. She's delightful and he's like a walking, talking, nightmare come to life. Oh my god, he's the present day Freddy! I really gotta find a way to take that guy out.

We get in our chauffeured car to head back to the docks and

when the driver closes the door I'm instantly on edge. Something is wrong.

"Your Majesty... Is it just me, or was our driver blonde earlier?" I take a look around to see if I can notice any other differences.

"Yeah, he was. Why?" He pulls himself out of whatever internal debate he was having with himself now that he's noticed I'm on edge.

"Because the guy that just tucked us into *this* car has black hair. And take notice, the seats have navy detailing, not black on black. This is definitely not our car. Something is wrong with this. Send a text to the guys and SB. Let them know my necklace is on please, because it'll take some time for the boys to get off the island, and Ren is working so he may not even have his phone turned on still. Don't touch or drink anything. Just hold me like you'll never let me go and we'll make the best of our time together. Whatever's about to happen is going to happen, but for now, it looks like we are going for a little ride."

Our car drives like it's going to the docks, but we pass the exit we'd need to get back to our boat. Matteo is nuzzling my neck, like he isn't watching everything like a hawk, but I know he's preparing himself for the worst.

No one messaged him back after his message went out, but we didn't expect responses. Everyone will jump into action as needed. I'm not worried about that. I'm worried about the unknown variables.

Who has taken us. What do they want? Blah, blah, blah... Am I going to have to listen to some inane villain speech? How do I keep Matteo safe? This likely has nothing to do with him and everything to do with me. Especially if this is his dad's doing.

Lorenzo is a selfish, narcissistic shitbag, but he needs his legacy to live on and Matteo is his only known heir. He wouldn't hurt him. At least, that's what I'm hoping. You never really know with psychopaths.

I lean into 'Teo's sweet kisses along my neck. He traces some of the marks left behind by the guys with his tongue, and it causes shivers to run down my spine. His touch is keeping me grounded. His warmth is keeping me sane.

My mind is moving a million miles per minute with thoughts of what's about to go down, but his touch brings me clarity and peace. It doesn't matter what's about to happen. I will stay calm and I will destroy anyone who tries to hurt Matteo. Period.

"Whatever is about to happen, good or bad, just know that I love you. I know what you're willing to do to keep me safe, but I want you to play this smart. Don't react to anything, especially if it has to do with me."

"It's okay, beautiful. I'm not worried. I love you too. Just remember how brutal you are when you want to be. When we get where we're going, you'll show them all. Did you bring your weapons?" I nod my head in response and he chuckles darkly.

"You're nothing if not my savage queen. I pity anyone who fucks with you or anyone you love. Don't underestimate anyone, but always remember who you are. Be a queen. Stay a savage. No one can take that away from you, though many will try." He kisses and bites my ear after his deep gravelly voice resonates through my entire being. Fuck he's damn hot when he wants to be.

Be a queen. Stay a savage.

I like that. Pulling his face up to meet mine, I kiss him. It's not one of those over the top extra kisses. It's simple and sweet and says "I love you always" with a light touch of my tongue against his. I savor the taste of our wine from dinner on his lips and sigh happily when the kiss stops.

"How did I get so lucky? I hope you never leave me." I whisper my fears into his neck, taking my time to return the favor with the kisses and caresses while nuzzling into him like he's my safe space.

It's pitch black wherever we are. The only lights, I imagine, are coming from the headlights on the car, but I can't even see that. The drive took us about an hour beyond where we were supposed to be but turned into long stretches of backroads at some point so it's safe to say we are in nowheres-ville USA.

The bulletproof separation partition has been up the entire drive, so we can't see or speak to the driver. The doors and windows appear to have the child's lock enabled so we can't get out unless we are let out.

Not that I mind being trapped with 'Teo, in fact, I'm actually enjoying it. It's no sweat off my back for me to sit here, comfortably wrapped up in the arms of my man trading kisses and sweet whispers to each other while being driven around and waiting for my other men to show up.

Although it would be nice to have an idea of what we're looking forward to. At this point, all signs point to us being fucked. Not by each other, and not in a good way. We are living out a real life scene from a horror movie and everything is about to go bad. I know this without having to guess who's behind it all. Getting creepily taken out to the woods mysteriously will likely never end well. No matter who's running the show.

I'm not really that worried. I think if anything I'm more annoyed that they are cutting into my special date night. I'll be downright pissed the fuck off if any of my guys get hurt.

At this point, this may very well be the most laid back kidnapping I've ever been a part of, so if their goal was to rattle me with the creepy drive, then they aren't very good bad guys. They don't even get points for creativity since this all feels pretty "by the book". Even 'Teo looks calm and happy.

"Why are you smiling? We've been kidnapped. You know this right?" I smile up at him in amusement.

"Well, yeah... But this time, I've been kidnapped *with* you. So at least I don't have to worry about the what if's. I'll gladly get stolen if it's with you." He deadpans, and I can't help it when the tears start rolling down my face - my laughter starts causing my sides to ache. He said it so seriously that I believe him. This crazy asshole *is* happy to be hijacked, because at least this time he knows he's here to keep me safe. That's how his mind really works. He looks at me with so much amusement and love shining in his eyes and I find myself, once again so thankful to have these perfect men in my life.

I'm still laughing when we roll to a stop. I'm wiping the happy tears from my eyes when the door opens. I snort another laugh out when the driver holds his hand out for me, like we're at a five star establishment instead of a giant brick building in the middle of nowhere. This place even looks like the ultimate bad guy location. Perfect for spilling and cleaning up the messes left behind from the mob life.

"Eh, I'm good Joe. I've got a hand to hold." I say as I pull myself out of the car and wait patiently for Matteo's hand.

"My name isn't Joe." He says to me, like it matters. Fun fact, it doesn't. Nothing about this guy is worth remembering.

"Don't care. What are we doing here?" I ask, thankful I already had the forethought to move my knife from my boot and made sure it's tucked away, concealed in the waistband of my pants.

"You're here to meet the boss. He doesn't take kindly to tardiness so let's move." He says, giving me a little shove into Matteo, causing the big man to growl.

"Calm my love, just breathe." I say only for 'Teo's ears.

"Hands to yourself, hot stuff or I'll have to let the big guy off his leash." I wink, provoking him further. The lower level guys usually aren't well known for their composure or capability of handling things without another person telling them what to do.

"Listen bitch-" Aaaand I'm done. I swing my leg around, landing a solid kick into the guy's chest.

Catching an opponent off guard is always my favorite. Men think that because of my size, I can't whoop their asses. Ha, fooled you mother fucker.

I throw myself on top of him and knock him out cold with a few hard knocks to the face. Then, just to be safe, I stab him in both arms, the gut and both legs. Doing a quick sweep for weapons, I pull his gun and hand it to Matteo. He doesn't have anything else on him so we leave him there to either bleed out or run away when he wakes up.

TWENTY-FIVE

ALESSANDRA

WE MAKE our way into the building, checking everything out to make sure we've got all of our bases covered. Knowing where the exits are never hurt anyone. From the looks of things, this is just a big empty warehouse. It's genuinely just a brick building with concrete floors and concrete walls. We walk in on the first level, but it looks as though there's a basement level as well and if anyone's in here, that's where they'll be.

I suppose we could've left after I took out the low level bitch outside, but where's the fun in that? If anything, it'll just make whoever is behind this come at us harder next time and to be honest, I'd rather just take care of everything now.

Matteo stays close on my heels, protecting me from behind as I make my way down the stairs, it opens up into a big dark room, and when I see one singular light bulb lit, dangling from the ceiling, it directs my attention to a man gagged and tied up to a lone metal chair in the middle of the room. His head is bent down low so his chin touches his chest as blood drips down from his temple and is pooling on the cement floor at his feet.

I know that man. I love that man... That guy knocked out and bleeding all alone in the middle of the room is Ren. It takes every last ounce of control not to rush him and make sure he's still breathing. My entire being is drawn to him like a moth to a flame, and if I go to him now, I fall into the trap and we all get burned.

Clap. Clap. Clap.

The clapping sounds from the farthest corner from me, shrouded in darkness. My skin prickles in goosebumps when I recognize the nauseating voice that accompanies the clapping.

"Ah, very good, mi amore. Not reacting to the 'love of your life' being held hostage and beaten within an inch of his life. You are most impressive. From an outside perspective one might believe you don't care for him at all. Especially since you can't manage to be faithful to him." He glares past me to Matteo and instinctively, I put my body directly in front of his. That awful voice calling me Ren's pet name for me almost makes me throw up, but I will not cower to this piece of shit.

"What the fuck Raffaele? What have you done?" I seethe.

"What? This? My grandson can take far more than this small beating. He's been trained for this. Actually this entire set up is entirely for your benefit. Something to improve the visual aesthetic if you will." The sadistic gleam in his eye can't be my imagination. He's getting off on the mystery and control he has in this situation.

"Excuse me? You did all of this for me? Because... I'm dating more than one guy? Do you have some sick fetish that we're playing out here or something? Oh, I get it, you were hoping for a place in my harem. Sorry, all the positions have been filled. Indefinitely."

"Tsk, tsk, you need to learn to watch your mouth around your superiors or you might find yourself dead... Or worse." He cocks his gun and aims it directly at Ren's head and I lose every bit of breath I have left in me.

"Calm my love. Just breathe." Matteo echoes my words back to me from outside, and I wonder if I'd be able to actually breathe if he weren't here reminding me, calming me.

I hear the click of another gun behind us, and I just know there's a big ugly goon holding a gun to the head of my other love. Shit. Fuck. God-motherfucking-damnit! We get pushed out into the open, only stumbling slightly, but still refusing to show fear. My will to keep them alive is much stronger than their want to play some stupid power play games.

"What do you want Raffaele?" I ask, letting a calm bravado take over. I walk to Ren and trace a finger down his cheek, wishing like hell he'd wake up, but also thankful he's knocked out so he doesn't have to play witness to whatever comes next.

"Well my dear, I'm sure you're well aware that no one lives to disrespect the Gavino name. Not even a Gavino. It appears as though you've managed to brainwash my grandson here into thinking that he's alright with sharing you with three other men. Let me assure you, that has not ever been acceptable and it never will be. He's as much a disgrace as you are a whore it would seem. You have two options here, because I love my grandson and I'm feeling generous." He cocks his head at me, like he's studying me. Watching to see what hints I'll give him to an insider perspective of my brain. Fat fucking chance old man.

"Pfft. Clearly you love your grandson. You show your affections well." I roll my eyes.

"Watch your smart mouth before you find my well of generosity has all dried up." He glares at me, as if that's enough to scare me into submission. This guy is intimidating, sure. But I'm not your average bitch. He made sure of it by forcing me to grow up in abject poverty, surrounded by drug addicts and rapists.

"As lovely as this trip has been, would you mind getting to your point? I'm getting tired. It's far past my bedtime." I smirk.

"You really can't help yourself can you? You're really just that ignorant, or maybe just that uncaring that your life hangs in the balance of all this." He says, genuine curiosity coloring his words.

"How about we up the stakes further? Hmm?" He nods to his goon and I can tell by the low grunt behind me that he's just done something to Matteo. I fight my instinct to tighten up or flinch. My body has to remain calm and unaffected in order to give this man nothing. The internal war waging in my mind is a direct contrast to my outward appearance.

"What are my options Raffaele? I wasn't lying when I said I'm growing tired. I don't like these silly power moves on a good day, and it just so happens that I'm incredibly sleep deprived this evening."

"Fine, let's move this along then so the little princess can get her beauty sleep then." He smiles, though it isn't a nice smile at all. Though whatever happens behind me wipes the smile from his lips in an instant. He lifts his gun and aims behind me. Without thinking I rush at him, unwilling to let him hurt Matteo.

"These boys just blindly follow you huh. Would they still if they knew you were married to Ren?! Would they settle for never being anything other than second best?!" And then he shoots me with a snarl on his lips.

Everything sort of slows down after that. I hear the bang of another gun. I see Raffaele's brain matter explode. I turn to see three of my kings standing tall and furious - not even bothering to come to me. I can't blame them after Raffaele sharing my secret with them like that. The throat of the man who hurt Matteo is slit and he lies dead on the floor and Ren is still knocked out cold.

And then I see nothing but darkness. There is no more light, there is no more love, but mostly there is no more pain. Instead I just sort of fade away...

ABOUT THE AUTHOR

Ali is a caffeine obsessed mama with a deep love of reading. Born and raised in Oregon, she loves to go on outdoor adventures with her family to rivers, lakes, mountains, walking trails and everything else along the way. She's got a special place in her heart for traveling and seeing new things, but most importantly, eating different foods from around the world. Her and her husband try to travel around the U.S to see at least one NFL game per year and at least one NBA game per year, but her favorite teams to watch are within her hometown when her kids play a new sport each season.

In her downtime, you can find Ali with a book or kindle in hand reading everything from lighthearted rom-coms to the dangerous and dirty world of dark romance. Add in some paranormal, a good thriller or mystery and she'll find herself lost for days in the hidden adventures within a good story. With words being her outlet and her sanity, she's decided to take a chance on herself and do a little more than just read. With her first book now published, she's fully immersing herself into the wonderful world of literature and has many more books planned to come. Keep your eye out for what she'll do next!

If you'd like to stalk her to find out more information on her upcoming releases, check out her social media.

www.ingramcontent.com/pod-product-compliance
Lightning Source LLC
Chambersburg PA
CBHW020926160726
47993CB00005B/2151